"I see marriage as the best solution to your problem."

Totally shocked, Stella struggled for breath. "Are you telling me you want to marry me off to someone?"

Callum gave the faintest of nods.

"How dare you?" She jumped to her feet. This wasn't something she could take sitting down. "So, who's the poor sucker you think I should trap into marriage?"

There was a beat of time before he said, very simply, "I am."

Barbara Hannay was born in Sydney, educated in Brisbane and has spent most of her adult life living in tropical north Queensland, where she and her husband have raised four children. While she has enjoyed many happy times camping and canoeing in the bush, she also delights in an urban lifestyle— chamber music, contemporary dance, movies and dining out. An English teacher, she has always loved writing, and now, by having her stories published, she is living her most cherished fantasy.

Look out for Gabe and Piper's story coming soon:
A Wedding at Winderoo (#3794)
In Harlequin Romance®, on sale April 2004

A BRIDE AT BIRRALEE
Barbara Hannay

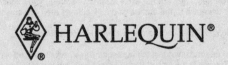

TORONTO • NEW YORK • LONDON
AMSTERDAM • PARIS • SYDNEY • HAMBURG
STOCKHOLM • ATHENS • TOKYO • MILAN • MADRID
PRAGUE • WARSAW • BUDAPEST • AUCKLAND

ISBN 0-373-03786-4

A BRIDE AT BIRRALEE

First North American Publication 2004.

Copyright © 2002 by Barbara Hannay.

This edition published by arrangement with Harlequin Books S.A.

® and TM are trademarks of the publisher. Trademarks indicated with ® are registered in the United States Patent and Trademark Office, the Canadian Trade Marks Office and in other countries.

Visit us at www.eHarlequin.com

Printed in U.S.A.

CHAPTER ONE

SOMEONE was coming.

Callum Roper slouched against a veranda post and glared at the distant cloud of dust. In the outback, dust travelling at that speed meant one thing—a vehicle heading this way.

He wasn't in the mood for visitors.

Turning his back on the view, he lowered his long body into a deep canvas chair and snapped the top off a beer. He took a deep swig and scowled. Truth was, he wasn't in the mood for anything much these days! Even beer didn't taste the same.

'Why'd you have to do it, Scotty?'

He hadn't meant to ask the question out loud, but there it was, lingering like the dust on the hot, still air. *Why did you have to go and die? Damn you, Scotty.*

Taking another, deeper swig, he grimaced. How long did it last, this grief business? His younger brother had been dead for six weeks now and he still felt as raw and hurt as he had the day the helicopter crashed and he'd first glimpsed Scott's lifeless body in the cockpit.

Slumping lower in the canvas seat, he reached for the cattle dog at his side and rubbed the soft fur between its ears, willing himself to relax. But a picture of Scott's sun-streaked curls, laughing brown eyes and cheeky grin swam before him. It was the face of an irrepressible larrikin. And it had gone for ever.

Late afternoons like this were the worst. This was the time of day he and Scott used to sit here on the veranda, having a beer and a yarn. His brother had been such damn good company. Drinking alone without Scott's humorous recounts of their day wasn't any kind of fun.

He cast a bitter glance over his shoulder towards the encroaching vehicle. Entertaining visitors without Scott's easy banter would be hell!

Luckily, cars didn't foray into these parts very often. Birralee Station was beyond Cloncurry in far north-western Queensland, further outback than most people liked to venture.

But this particular cloud of dust was definitely edging closer down the rust-red track. He could hear the motor now and it sounded tinny, not the throaty roar of the off-road vehicles his neighbours used.

Surely no one with any sense would come all the way out here in a flimsy little city sedan? City visitors were even worse than well-meaning neighbours.

Scott had been the one for the city. He'd always been flying off to Sydney or Brisbane to seek out fun and female company. Callum was content to stick to the bush, restricting his socialising to picnic races and parties on surrounding properties. He'd never felt the urge to go chasing off to the city.

Almost never. His hand tightened around the beer can as a reluctant memory forced him to acknowledge that there had been one city woman he'd wanted to chase. A woman with crow black hair, a haunting, sexy voice and a gutsy, shoulders-back attitude. He'd wanted to chase her, catch her and brand her as his.

But his little brother had always had the happy knack of smiling at a girl in a certain way and rendering her smitten. Instantly. Accepting that the woman he'd desired had preferred Scott had been a bitter lesson.

Hell! What was the use of sitting here, thinking about all that again?

Callum jumped to his feet and frowned as he realised the car had stopped. He squinted at the stretch of bushland before him, searching for the tell-tale dust. Late afternoon sun lent a bronze glow to the paddocks of pale Mitchell grass, but there was no sign of movement. The cloudless sky, the trees and grass, even the cattle, were as still as a painting.

Crossing to the edge of the veranda, he stood listening. All he could hear now was the high, keening call of a black falcon as it circled above the cliff on the far side of the creek.

He frowned. By his calculations, the car had been close to the creek crossing. Perhaps the driver had stopped to check the water's depth before fording the shallow stream.

Leaning forward, he rested his elbows on the veranda railing and listened, watched and waited.

A good five minutes or more passed before the engine started up again. But when it did, it screamed and strained. Then there was silence again, before another useless burst from the motor.

'Silly sod's got himself bogged.' He listened for a few more minutes. There was more high-pitched whirring from the straining motor. More silence.

Shaking his head, he let out a heavy sigh. The last thing he felt like was playing hero to some uninvited city slicker, but he could hardly ignore the fact that someone seemed to be having car trouble so close to his homestead.

He had no choice. Cursing softly, he loped down the front steps and across the gravel drive to his ute.

Stella knew she was bogged. She was down to her axle in loose pebbles and sand in the middle of the outback—the middle of *nowhere*—and she was sick as a dog, more miserable than a lost puppy.

Another wave of nausea rose from her stomach to her mouth and she sat very still, willing her stomach to settle. It probably hadn't been very bright to stop in the middle of the creek, but she'd felt so ill she'd had no choice.

How hard was this going to get? She'd been in enough mess before she'd left home, but now she was stuck in this crummy little creek hundreds of kilometres from anywhere—and out of the mobile network. When she needed to phone Scott, she couldn't!

It was her own fault, of course. She should have tried ringing him again before she'd left Sydney and told him she was coming. Then he would have given her detailed directions. He might have warned her about this creek crossing.

But if she'd rung him, he would have expected to know why she wanted to see him. And she hadn't liked to explain about the baby over the phone.

After their breakup, she *couldn't* have discussed her pregnancy over the phone. There was just too much to talk about and it was all too complicated. She wanted to work out the very best solution for their baby's future, and to do that she needed to discuss it with him face to face.

And she hadn't wanted to waste precious money on air fares when she might need it for the baby, so she'd spent five days—nearly a week—driving all this way from Sydney.

Sighing heavily, she looked at her watch and then at the reddening sky. It would be dark soon and, for the first time since she'd left home, she felt genuinely frightened.

Fighting off the urge to panic, she forced herself to consider her options. She couldn't spend the night sleeping in the car in the middle of an outback creek; and trying to make camp under trees up on the bank had no appeal. No, she'd rather gamble on how far she was from the homestead and try to walk from here.

She reached into the back of her little car and groped for her shoes, but before she could find them the sound of a motor came throbbing towards her.

Her head shot up and she peered through the dust-streaked windscreen. Silhouetted against the sun, a utility truck crested the low hill on the other side of the creek, then rattled effortlessly down the dirt- and gravel-strewn slope.

'Thank you, God.' Smiling with relief, she dropped her shoe and her spirits soared as she watched the ute rumble towards her over the loose, water-washed rocks in the creek-bed. Perhaps it was Scott driving. 'Please, let it be Scott.'

There was a male figure at the wheel and a blue heeler cattle dog perched on the seat next to him.

The truck pulled to a halt beside her.

From her little low car, she looked up. The driver's face was shaded by the brim of his akubra hat, but she saw black stubble on a resolute jaw and dark hair on a strongly muscled forearm.

Not Scott. Oh, dear, no. Not Scott, but the one man she'd hoped to avoid. His brother, Callum.

Stella's breathing snagged and she lowered her gaze. *Callum!* This was a moment she'd dreaded, and she hadn't expected to have to deal with it right at the start.

She wet her lips and looked up at him with her chin at a defiant angle. 'Hi, Callum.'

He didn't answer.

'I—I'm afraid I'm stuck.'

The truck's door squeaked as he shoved it open. With an excessive lack of haste, his well-worn, brown leather riding boots lowered into the shallow creek. The boots were followed by an endless pair of blue jeans, a faded blue cotton shirt that stretched wide across powerful shoulders and, finally, a dark unsmiling face beneath a broad-brimmed hat.

It was a face she hadn't seen for twelve months. A face that still haunted her secret dreams. Dreams she never dared think about in the light of day.

For an agonisingly long moment, he didn't speak. He stood still as a mountain, his thumbs hooked through the loops of his jeans. 'What the hell are you doing here?'

What a beast! No greeting. No, How do you do, Stella? Long time, no see, or, Can I help? Not a trace of polite concern. Not even G'day.

For a heartbeat, she wondered if Callum Roper had forgotten her? That would be convenient but, short of his developing amnesia, she didn't think it was possible for him to have forgotten *that* party. Nevertheless, she deserved a warmer greeting than this!

At least when she found Scott and told him about getting bogged, *he* would be sympathetic.

She remained sitting in her car and held out her hand. It was about time this oaf was forced to remember his manners. 'How are you, Callum?'

Their eyes met. His expression was so fierce and hard that she knew, even before he spoke, that he hadn't forgotten her.

'Stella.' He nodded and grunted an incomprehensible greeting. After just a trace of hesitation, his big hand closed around hers.

It was the hard, callused hand of an outdoors man and she tried to ignore the goose-bumps that rushed up her arms in response to such simple contact. This was Scott's brother, her baby's uncle, and she really would have to learn to relax when he was around.

Easier said than done.

'You're asking for trouble if you stop in the middle of a creek,' he said.

Damn him. 'I didn't deliberately get myself bogged, you know. You should have a sign warning people about this creek.'

'If there was any sign, it would warn trespassers they'd be prosecuted,' Callum growled as he circled her car slowly, hoping his shock didn't show.

His heart was racing at a hectic gallop. The last thing he'd expected to find had been this particular woman stranded on his property. What the hell was *she* doing here?

Silly question. His stomach dropped like a leg-roped steer as he acknowledged there could only be one reason. She'd come to see Scott. Hell! She didn't know.

His brother hadn't shared details about his recent trips to the city, and Callum hadn't asked. He'd never even known for sure if Scott and Stella had still been an item, and she wasn't family, she wasn't a close friend, so he hadn't sent her word of the accident. At least that was the excuse he'd rationalised.

How the blue blazes could he tell her now?

He was uncomfortably aware of her cool grey eyes assessing him as he checked how far her wheels had sunk into the silty creek-bed. Only a class act like Stella Lassiter could look dignified in such a predicament.

Perhaps her dignity came from the way she kept her chin haughtily high as she sat quietly in her car. Or maybe it was an impression created by that broad, full mouth that made her look earthy rather than vulnerable. Maybe it was all that shiny hair, black as a witch's cat.

'How does it look? Am I salvageable?' she called. Her voice was another problem. Smooth and low, it had a syrupy cadence that kicked him at gut level and conjured a host of images he'd tried so hard to forget.

Hell, maybe she was a witch. In a matter of moments, some soft segment of his brain seemed to be slipping under her spell. *Just like last time!*

He forced his thoughts to practicalities. Her ridiculous little toy car was well and truly bogged, but it would be easy enough to haul her out.

Reaching into the back of his ute, he grabbed the D shackle and snatchem strap. 'Sit tight,' he ordered sharply and bent to shackle the long strap to a low bracket on the front of her car. 'I'll give you a tow.'

Leaping high into the truck again, he backed it around until it was positioned in front of hers and then, out of the ute once more, he looped the other end of the strap over the ball joint on his tow bar.

She opened her car door and leaned out to watch what he was doing. And Callum found himself staring at her feet as she sat in her car's open doorway with the skirt of her light cotton dress bunched over her knees and her bare feet propped on the doorway's rim.

Her feet were exquisitely shaped. Each neat toe was topped by perfectly applied, sky-blue nail polish. A fine silver chain threaded with blue glass beads was secured neatly around one dainty ankle.

Callum couldn't drag his eyes away. Her feet were as interesting and compelling as the rest of her.

Suddenly, she drew her legs into the car and pulled the door smartly shut. Had he been gaping? Perhaps he was more of a country hick than he realised. Through the window, she studied him and chewed her full bottom lip, showing a trace of vulnerability for the first time. 'I've come to see Scott. I hope he's home,' she said.

Callum swallowed. He knew she'd come looking for Scott and he should have been thinking about that instead of gaping at her mouth and her hair and her *feet!*

'Ah—' a painful constriction dammed his throat '—I'm—er—I'm afraid you're going to be disappointed. Scott's—' *Stuff this!* He avoided looking at her as he blinked stinging eyes. 'Scott's not here.'

'What?' She stared at him, her eyes wide with disbelief and despair. 'Where is he?' Her strength seemed to leave her suddenly. She looked crumpled and crestfallen. 'I've— I've driven all the way from Sydney. I've got to see him.'

Callum shot a hopeless glance to the darkening sky. If it hadn't been so late in the day, he would have considered breaking the bad news and sending her packing! But there was less than half an hour of daylight left.

Forcing her to go back down the rough Kajabbi track in the dark wasn't an option. Chances were she'd get bogged again, or even worse she could hit a deep rut and turn this little death trap over.

'I'll tow you out of here and you'd better follow me up to the homestead,' he said.

'Thanks.' Her reply came in a whisper and she looked very pale, as if the stuffing had been knocked right out of her. 'But can I contact Scott from there?'

Callum cleared his throat. 'It'll be easier to explain about Scott when we get back to the house.'

Without waiting to see her reaction, he spun on his heel and climbed back into the ute, calling over his shoulder, 'Let your handbrake off and don't turn your engine on yet. Just leave it in neutral.'

He edged the truck forward and the creek-bed released her car easily. After towing her to the top of the small rise, he stopped while he unhitched the vehicles. 'The home-stead's only a kilometre down the track. See you there.' Without looking her way again, he accelerated around a bend and headed for Birralee.

Scott wasn't here. It was more than she could bear. Stella fought to stay calm as she guided her little car over the last twists and turns of the bumpy track. She'd been keeping all her worries to herself for too long, but she couldn't hold on much longer.

She had never been one for confiding in her friends and the events of the past few months had snowballed into an unbearable, secret burden. First, when she'd realised that Scott hadn't been as committed to their relationship as she'd believed, there had been the unpleasantness of the breakup.

Then she'd discovered she was pregnant!

She'd almost lost the plot when she'd learned that, but after taking time to get used to the idea she'd tried to contact Scott. The message on his answering machine had said he would be out mustering the back blocks of Birralee for several weeks.

The final blow had fallen with a phone call from London and the job offer of her dreams! A British television network wanted to hire her skills as a meteorologist to head the research for a series of documentaries about global warming in Europe.

She couldn't believe the bad timing!

She'd studied so hard and had worked her socks off in the hope of scoring a contract like this, but the amount of travel involved and the primitive living conditions required on location meant it wasn't a job for a woman with a tiny baby.

If only she and Scott had been more careful! But there'd

been too many laughs…too much country-boy charm…too many empty assurances that she really was the one and only woman for him…

Stella knew they were poor excuses. She was educated. She was a scientist! She knew better! But…for the first time in her life, she'd allowed herself to let go…

She'd let herself be just a little like her mother. And, just like her mother, her mistakes had caught her out.

She carried the consequences within her. The cluster of little cells, multiplying rapidly every day. Oh, God! She'd been carrying the secret burden of her pregnancy for four lonely months now and she couldn't keep it to herself any longer.

She had to speak to Scott.

The job offer had been too wonderful to resist and so she'd accepted it, but she couldn't fulfil her contract without Scott's help. *Scott, where are you? At the very least, I need to talk this through with someone.*

Ahead of her, Callum had pulled up in front of a typical outback homestead. She'd never visited one before, but she was familiar with the image—a low and sprawling timber house with a ripple-iron roof and deep verandas set in the middle of an expanse of lawn and shaded by ancient trees.

So this was Scott's home—Birralee. This was where the father of her baby had been born. He'd run on this grass as a little boy. He was at home in this wild, rough country with its rocky red cliffs, its haze of soft green bush and its vast wide plains, so flat you could see the curvature of the earth as you drove across them.

And of course this was Callum's home, too.

He stood waiting, his blue heeler squatting obediently beside him. His face remained fierce and unsmiling as she parked her car on the grass next to his truck. He'd taken his hat off and she saw the tangle of his dark, rough curls and the golden brown lights that might soften his eyes if he'd let them.

Callum had never looked very much like Scott. Where Scott was blond and boyish, full of sunshine and laughter, Callum was darker and older, more stormy and grim. OK…she had to admit he was still good-looking in his own hard way.

Who was she trying to kid? Callum was incredibly good-looking. Heaven knew, she'd been attracted to him from the very first moment she'd laid eyes on him. But he had a dangerous brand of good looks that fascinated yet unnerved her. There was a magnetic fierceness about Callum that pierced hidden depths in her and threatened her inner peace.

She'd recognised a perilous intensity in him on the night they'd met…

Get a grip! You'll be a complete mess if you think about that now!

Hopefully, she wouldn't have to spend too much time around him. She needed inner peace more than ever now. She needed cheering up.

She needed Scott.

Where was Scott? Why hadn't Callum told her straight away where he was? Her stomach churned and her smile was grim as she climbed out of her little car and stretched cramped limbs.

'Do you have much gear?' Callum asked.

'Just one bag and a bird cage.'

'A bird cage?' He didn't try to hide his surprise.

Her chin lifted. 'I had to bring my bird. My flatmate's absolutely hopeless about remembering to change Oscar's seed or water. Last time I left him with her, the poor darling nearly dehydrated.'

Carefully, she extracted the cage from the back of her

car and eyed his cattle dog warily as she made introductions. 'This is Oscar.'

Callum scowled at the little blue budgerigar.

'What's your dog's name?'

Her question seemed to surprise him. 'Mac,' he muttered.

At the sound of his name, Mac's ears pricked and he sprang to his feet, tail wagging madly.

'Hi, Mac.' She shot Callum a cautious glance. 'He doesn't like to nip at small birds, does he?'

He cracked a brief smile. 'He's a true blue heeler. From when he was a pup he knew that his mission in life was to nip at the heels of cattle. I doubt he's ever paid any attention to birds.'

'That's a relief.'

Callum scruffed the top of the dog's head. 'Poor old fella's retired to home duties these days.'

Stella saw Callum's genuine affection for his dog and she felt a tiny bit better. Somehow it helped to know that the grim Callum Roper was as fond of his pet as she was of hers.

His smile faded as he nodded his head towards the house. 'You bring the bird cage. I'll grab your bag.'

'Thanks.' Reaching back into the car, she fished out her shoes and slipped her feet into them. Then, puzzled and curious, she followed the dog and his master up three wide wooden steps.

As Callum led her along the veranda, she couldn't help noticing that he made an art form of the loose-hipped, long-legged saunter of the outback cattleman.

With an easy dip of one broad shoulder, he pushed a door open. 'You'll have to stay here tonight, so you'd better have this room.' He stepped aside to let her enter, then placed her bag with surprising care on top of a carved sandalwood box at the foot of the bed.

She dragged her attention from him to the room. It was old-fashioned and simply furnished. There was no personal clutter and it was very clearly a guest room. The floor-boards were left uncovered and the big double bed had brass ends and was covered by a patchwork quilt in various shades of green and white.

On the wall was a painting of a stormy sky and horses galloping down a steep mountainside with their manes and tails flying.

'I'm afraid I'm imposing on your hospitality.'

He didn't answer, but his gaze dropped to the bird cage she was still holding.

'I'll put this out on the veranda,' she suggested.

'You'd better bring it through to the kitchen. Mac won't touch it, but if you leave it outside the possums might knock it over during the night.'

'Really?'

A hint of mischief danced in his eyes. 'Or a carpet snake might fancy a midnight snack.'

'Oh, no!' Horrified, she clutched the cage to her. 'I'd be grateful if he could stay in the kitchen, thank you.'

Once again, she followed Callum's long strides. This time down a long hall with polished timber floorboards and rooms opening off its entire length.

Where was Scott? An uneasy tension coiled in her stomach. She hoped she wasn't going to be sick. The hardest part of her journey was still ahead of her.

When she found Scott, not only did she have to tell him he was going to be a father, she had to convince him that the plan she'd agonised over really was the best solution.

Best for him and the baby and for her.

It was a straightforward plan. She would resign from

her current job, have the baby and then Scott would look after it while she went to London. Luckily the television project was so big that the company did their recruiting well in advance. She was due to give birth several weeks before her contract started and after twelve months she would come back and take over her responsibilities as a mother.

As she headed down the hall, she prayed that Scott would see the beautiful simplicity and fairness of what she was asking. If only she didn't feel so scared!

The rooms she glimpsed as she hurried after Callum were a little shabby, a little untidy, decidedly old-fashioned, but she had an impression of tasteful decor and comfort and an easy, unpretentious air that made them welcoming. Easy to live in.

Easy and charming like Scott had been. She could imagine him here. But could she imagine leaving his baby here at this house? Could she really leave a tiny baby way out here in the never-never while she spent a year overseas?

Everything depended on Scott's reaction.

And maybe Callum's.

They reached the kitchen at the back of the house. It was huge and cluttered and Stella fell in love with it at first sight.

The reaction was so unexpected. All her life, she'd been walking into other people's kitchens. There'd been a bewildering series of them during her childhood—dingy council flats, women's shelters and foster homes. Until she'd moved into the little flat she shared with Lucy, she'd never lived in one place for very long. Their kitchen was neat and trendy, but she'd never felt an immediate rapport with a room the way she did now.

She loved it. Loved the long wall of deep, timber-framed windows of clear glass with dark green diamond panes in the middle, pushed wide open to catch the breeze. Loved the spellbinding views of the twilight-softened bush as it dipped down to the creek and climbed on the other side to majestic red cliffs in the distance.

She loved the huge scrubbed pine table in the middle of the room, home to a wonderful jumble of odd bits and pieces—a flame-coloured pottery bowl overflowing with dried gum nuts, a pile of *Country Life* magazines, a horse's bridle and several bulging packets of photographs.

The collection of unmatched chairs gathered around the table enchanted her. With no effort at all, she could picture these chairs seating a party of happy, chatting friends or family. She could almost hear their bright, laughter-filled voices.

Standing in the kitchen's corner, was an old timber high chair with scratched red paint. Stella couldn't help staring at it, wondering...

'You can park the bird cage on that high chair if you like,' Callum said. 'We only use it when my sisters bring their tribes to visit.'

She did as he suggested. 'There you go, Oscar. You can have a lovely view of the gum trees and talk to all the other birds outside.'

Callum's mouth twitched. 'You don't think he might get ideas about escaping?'

She glanced again at the bush and couldn't help wondering if Oscar craved for freedom to explore that vast sky and all those trees, but then she shoved that disagreeable thought aside. 'I look after him too well,' she assured Callum primly.

He walked to the fridge. 'Would you like a beer?'

'No. No, thanks.'

'Scotch, sherry, wine? I'm afraid I can't manage any fancy cocktails.'

'I won't have any alcohol, thank you.'

He seemed surprised. 'Cup of tea?'

'Yes, in a minute. That would be nice, but first, please, you must tell me about Scott. How can I contact him?'

He stiffened and she felt a stab of panic. His face seemed momentarily grey and he turned quickly away from her and snatched a beer out of the fridge.

What's the matter? What's wrong? Her heart began to thud.

'You'd better sit down,' he said without looking at her. 'I'm afraid I've got bad news about Scott.'

CHAPTER TWO

CALLUM fiddled with his unopened beer. His guts crawled with dread as he imagined Stella's reaction to his news.

Scott's dead. The words were so hard to get out.

Telling his parents had been the worst, the very worst moment of his life. Scott had been the baby of the family—everybody's favourite. To tell his mother and father had meant inflicting unbearable pain.

If Stella was in love with his brother, she was sure to burst into noisy tears. What the hell would he do then?

'Callum,' she said, and her voice vibrated with tension, 'I need to know what's happened to Scott.'

He realised he was still holding the beer, rolling it back and forth between anxious hands. The last thing he needed on this night was another beer. Hastily, he shoved it back in the fridge and cleared his throat.

'There was a mustering accident a few weeks back. Scott was flying a helicopter.'

She looked pale. Too pale. And she sat stiffly, without speaking, staring at him. Waiting.

'I'm afraid Scotty was killed.' He couldn't keep the tremor from his voice.

At first he thought she hadn't heard him. She just sat there, not making a sound, not moving.

After some time, she whispered, 'No! *No!* He can't be dead.'

He braced himself for the tears, eyeing the box of tissues on the bench to his right.

But she didn't cry. She just kept sitting there looking stunned, while her face turned from pale to greenish.

'I'm sorry to have to give you such bad news,' he said, wishing she didn't look so ill and wishing he didn't sound so clumsy and obviously uncomfortable. Wishing she would say something. *Anything.*

Her hand wavered to her mouth and for a moment he thought she was going to be sick.

'Are you OK?'

'I—I—' She tried to stand and swayed groggily before moaning faintly and collapsing back into her chair, her head slumped sideways.

'Stella.' Crouching quickly at her side, he touched her shoulder and to his relief she moved slightly. Her dark hair hung in a silky curtain hiding her face and, with two fingers, he lifted it away. Her eyes were shut and her skin was cool and pale.

Hell! She'd cared about Scott *this* much?

A hard knot of pain dammed his throat as he scooped her in his arms and, edging sideways through the kitchen doorway, carried her back to her room.

'I'm all right,' she protested weakly.

He didn't answer. Her pale fragility alarmed him. In his arms, she felt too light, too slim. *Too soft and womanly.* He drew in a ragged breath as her satiny, sweet-smelling hair brushed his neck. One shoe fell off as he made his way down the hallway, and he saw again the delicate foot with its pretty blue toenails, the gypsy-like allure of her dainty ankle chain.

His chest tightened with a hundred suppressed emotions as he laid her on the bed and removed the other shoe.

'Thank you,' she whispered. Her grey eyes opened and they held his. A trembling, thrilling, silent exchange passed between them. She looked away. 'I felt a little faint,' she said and tried to sit up.

It only took the slightest pressure of his fingers on her shoulders to push her back onto the bed. 'You've had a shock. Take it easy there for a minute or two.'

Lifting a crocheted rug from the chair in the corner, he spread it over her.

Outside it was almost dark. He switched on the shaded bedside lamp, then retrieved her shoe from the hallway, and when he returned her eyes were closed again and she seemed to be calmer.

For too long, Callum stood beside the bed, taking his fill of her special style of beauty. Noticing the way her eyelids were criss-crossed by a fine tracery of delicate blue veins and how very black her long lashes were against her pale cheeks. Heaven help him, he'd spent too many nights imagining her like this—in bed. What a silly damn fool he was.

He crossed to the French doors that opened onto the veranda and stood quietly, leaning against the door jamb, watching the bush grow dark, watching this woman who'd been looking for his brother. Wondering if her fainting spell had been caused by more than the shock of his news and thinking that perhaps a little crying would have been easier to handle after all.

The bush beyond the house grew still and silent. All day the birds had filled the air with their noisy chatter and screeches, but now they'd stopped calling, responding to the approach of night as if obeying an unseen conductor. Very soon the cicadas would tune in.

After some time, Stella's eyes opened and she rolled onto her side.

'How are you feeling now?'

Her eyebrows lifted in surprise when she saw him standing in the doorway. Elbow crooked, she propped up her head. 'I'm OK. Truly. But I can't believe that Scott—' Her eyes glistened, but no tears fell. 'It must have been so awful. Can you tell me what happened?'

He nodded slowly. 'We were out mustering in the rough country on the far western boundaries of this property. We needed to use the helicopter to chase some stragglers out of a gully and Scott flew in close and somehow the tail rotor clipped a gum tree.'

He didn't add that it had been his fault Scott had been flying that day. He kept that guilty secret to himself, let it gnaw away at his insides like white ants in a tree stump.

Sighing, he glanced again at the darkening bush beyond the veranda. 'It all happened very quickly.'

'So you were with Scott at the time?'

'No.' His chest squeezed so tight that for a moment he couldn't breathe. 'Scott insisted on going solo and he was having the time of his life. I was on horseback down below.'

He closed his eyes. There was still no way to block out the memory. The terror of the chopper going down. The crazy, lurching fall. The horrifying, screeching sound of ripping metal. The hellish moment of finding Scott, blood-soaked and slumped in the pilot's seat, staring back at him with blank, sightless eyes.

Hell! Each day it seemed to become more vivid.

'Why didn't you contact me, Callum?'

The challenge in her voice piqued his pride, spurring sudden anger. 'I wasn't my brother's keeper. I didn't keep tabs on his women. How was I to know you were still in the picture? I thought he'd taken up with some girl in Brisbane.'

She swung her gaze away and bit down hard on her lip and Callum wished he'd been less brutal. 'I would have let you know, but I didn't...' *Didn't want to be reminded that you'd chosen Scott over me...* His Adam's apple felt the size of a rock melon. 'It's a damn shame you had to come all this way—without knowing.'

Closing her eyes, she smiled wryly as she gave a faint shake of her head. 'It's a damn shame all right.' Her smoky deep voice resonated with bitter self-mockery.

Again he asked, 'How are you feeling?'

'Like a dill-brain.'

'I was referring to your stomach. Has it settled? I'll make a cup of tea, or perhaps you can manage a bite to eat?'

She pushed herself into a sitting position. 'I suppose I should try to eat.'

'I'll get dinner, then. I'm afraid it's only leftover stew.'

'Anything will be fine, thanks. I'm not really hungry.'

Callum left the room and Stella lay there, watching his broad, straight back. She tried not to think. Tried not to worry. Not to panic!

She was alone now. Totally alone. There was no one to turn to. Her bright dreams were dead. There would be no trip to London. No father for her baby. She couldn't dream of asking Callum to help. Her last hope had died with Scott.

Oh, God! Poor Scott! She shouldn't be feeling sorry for herself. He hadn't deserved to die. He'd been too young, too healthy, too brimming with energy and love of life.

How could Scott be dead?

Her mother had died when she was fifteen and her death had never seemed real. This was even harder to believe.

And poor Callum. How terrible for him to see his brother die in such a terrible accident. And how hard to carry on alone out here without him!

She pressed a hand to her slightly rounded stomach. Her poor little baby, already fatherless before it drew breath. That was the worst of all.

Just like her mother, she was producing a child who would never know its father. Although, unlike her mother, Stella was quite clear about her baby's paternity.

Her mother had never been sure. 'It was one of the lecturers at uni.,' she'd admitted once, just once, in a mismanaged attempt to be close to Stella. 'One of the nutty professors—but I don't know which.'

By contrast, there was only one man who could be the father of Stella's baby's. The fact that he was dead was too much to take in. Her insides shook with fear. Fear for herself, for the baby. Especially for the baby.

Scott was dead.

Where did that leave her? She couldn't stand being alone any longer. All her childhood, she'd felt lonely—handed from one adult to another. Life had always been hard.

As an adult, she'd found it easiest to bury herself in study. When she'd discovered science, she'd found the laws of physics to be true and unchanging. They never let her down. Which was more than she could say for the people in her life.

And she'd really wanted the job in London! It would have allowed her to apply her scientific knowledge to a fascinating project. She'd been so excited. But the television network wouldn't want a woman with a tiny baby. She'd really needed Scott's help.

With a shaky sigh, she swung her legs over the edge of the bed and stood up. The dizziness seemed to have passed. So far so good.

She made her way back through the house to the kitchen, knowing the only thing that would hold her together now was habit. Old habits died hard and she'd learned as a child that it was best not to let others see how worried she was about all the mess in her life.

In the kitchen, Callum had everything ready. With rough movements, he placed a plate of food in front of her. 'My version of outback hospitality.'

The meal smelt surprisingly good. Rich beef and vegetables. 'Mmm. Good wholesome country fare.'

'Just like mother used to make?' he asked as he took his seat and pushed a knife and fork across the table towards her.

Stella rolled her eyes. 'Not my mother.'

He frowned and waited, as if he expected her to clarify that remark. When she didn't, he said stiffly, 'I don't want to pry, but I'm assuming this visit to see Scott was rather important?'

She felt her cheeks grow hot. 'Not really. I—I had a few days spare and I just thought I'd look him up.'

His eyes told her he didn't believe her and his mouth thinned into a very straight line. 'So you'll be leaving again in the morning?'

She hadn't been ready for his question. Her head shot up making her look more haughty than she intended. 'Sure. I'll be out of your hair as soon as the sun comes up.'

Standing abruptly, he crossed back to the stove and filled the teapot with boiling water from the kettle. Stella bit her lip. Callum had been hospitable and she'd been rude. 'Do you live here by yourself now?' she asked, trying to make amends.

'Yes.' He thumped the lid onto the pot.

'How do you manage such a big property on your own?'

'I manage. My father tried to persuade me that the property's too big for one man. He wanted to send someone out to help me.'

'But you refused help?'

'I don't want anyone else here.' The message was loud and very clear.

'So how do you do it all?'

Callum turned from the stove and shrugged. 'It's not that difficult if you're prepared to work hard. And there are plenty of blokes looking for mustering contracts. I can hire a team of fencers if I need to.'

'You mentioned your sisters before. Do they live in these parts?'

One of his eyebrows rose quizzically. 'Didn't my little brother tell you about the family?'

Stella concentrated on her food. She didn't want to admit to Callum that there'd been disappointments in her relationship with Scott. She forced a nonchalant smile. 'It was tit for tat. I didn't tell Scott about my family either. We liked it that way.'

It was partly the truth. After she'd let Scott make love to her, she'd expected they would become closer in every way, that he'd begin to share more of his life with her. But the minute he'd sensed she'd been getting serious, he'd become edgy and had backed away.

Callum brought the teapot and mugs to the table. 'My mob don't have any secrets. Both my sisters married North Queensland graziers. Catherine lives on a property near Julia Creek and Ellie is just outside Cloncurry. They both love the bush life. They're happy as possums up a gum tree.'

'Do they have children?'

'Three kids apiece.'

'Wow. That's quite a family. It must be crowded when they all visit.'

'It's great.' His eyes glowed and he actually smiled. And

Stella wished he wouldn't. Callum Roper was far too attractive when his eyes lit up that way.

She glanced at Oscar in his cage in the corner. He was her family, the only living thing in the world that belonged to her. Apart from the baby. But the baby was invisible. Most of the time, she had trouble thinking of it as real.

Callum leaned back in his chair. 'And I suppose you know all about our old man?'

She frowned. 'Your father? Should I know about him?'

She was surprised when he almost laughed. 'He would like to think so, but then, all politicians have huge egos.'

'Politicians?' Stella almost dropped her fork. *Roper... Roper...* Was there a state politician named Roper? Suddenly she remembered. Not state government. Federal. 'Your dad is Senator Ian Roper?'

''Fraid so.'

'Oh, good grief!' In her head, she added a few swear words and the invisible cluster of cells in her body suddenly posed a whole new parcel of problems.

Just how much bad luck did a girl have to deal with? She was carrying the illegitimate grandchild of one of the country's most outspokenly conservative politicians!

Suddenly their efforts at conversation deteriorated. It seemed neither of them had much to say. Stella's curiosity about Scott's family vanished. She was back in panic mode again.

After they'd eaten, he asked, 'Are you feeling OK now?'

'Yes, much better, thank you. You're a great cook. Dinner was delicious.'

'Feel free to go straight to bed.'

'I'll help you clean up.'

His dark brows beetled in a deep frown. 'No, you won't.'

She had the distinct impression that he'd had enough of being sociable. He wanted her out of the room.

'You're sure I can't help?'

He nodded without speaking.

Standing slowly, she said, 'You'll be closing the kitchen windows, won't you?'

He frowned. 'I don't usually bother.'

'But—with Oscar in here—and the snakes and—everything.'

Callum almost grinned. 'Oh, yeah. The snakes. OK, I'll close the windows.'

CHAPTER THREE

STELLA was sick the next morning.

As Callum came back from the holding yards, striding through the dewy bluegrass with Mac at his heels, he heard unmistakable sounds coming from the bathroom.

They stopped him dead in his tracks. She was supposed to be heading off this morning. Leaving him in peace. But how could he send her packing if she was sick?

He kicked at a loose stone and sent it rolling down the incline. Instantly alert, the blue heeler watched its descent then seemed to decide it wasn't worth chasing.

Callum watched it, too, as it bounced from rock to rock before disappearing into the scrub on the creek bank. This sickness of Stella's was rather unusual. The fainting last night and now this…

Perhaps she had a simple stomach bug, but she'd woofed down that tucker last night without any problems. He frowned. That was how his sisters had been when they'd been expecting. Fine one minute, then suddenly dizzy or racing to the bathroom.

Was she pregnant? No, surely not.

His head shot back. She damn well could be pregnant.

The more he thought about it, the more he was sure he'd hit on the truth. Of course she was pregnant. That was why she'd hightailed it all the way from Sydney looking for Scott. That's why she'd been so upset.

Damn and blast you, little brother. What have you gone and done now?

If Stella was pregnant… If she was carrying Scott's

child… If she was planning on heading back to the city…disappearing again as quickly as she'd appeared…taking Scott's baby with her…

He slapped his palm against the rough trunk of a bloodwood tree and stared blankly into the distance, while tumultuous thoughts raged. Thoughts of Scott, of his family, of his own guilt and grief, his parents' heartbreak.

Thoughts of Scott in Stella's bed.

Groaning, he kicked another loose stone. Distasteful as it was, he had little choice; he had to ask her. If Scott was leaving behind a son or daughter, he needed to know.

Fists clenched, he turned reluctantly and marched towards the house.

Stella was in the kitchen, hovering in front of the stove and squinting at the dials. She was wearing denim cut-offs and a simple white T-shirt and her feet were bare except for the silver ankle chain with its blue glass beads.

She turned and smiled at him warily. 'Good morning.'

He nodded. 'Morning. Did you sleep well?'

'Like a log, thank you. I didn't realise how tired I was.' She pointed to the stove. 'I thought I'd make a cup of tea, but I haven't quite worked out how to drive your stove.'

'It's fairly straightforward,' he muttered.

'Uh-uh.' She shook her head. 'An electric kettle is straightforward. A stove this size requires a licence to operate. I'm surprised you have something so complicated way out in the bush.'

'We needed it when all the family lived at home.' He reached past her to flick appropriate switches. 'My mother takes her cooking seriously.'

Stella gave a wry grin as she shrugged. 'I'm afraid I'm a victim of the microwave era. If it doesn't light up with little messages telling me what to do, I'm lost.'

She ran slim fingers through her shiny black hair. Her

hands, like her feet, were elegantly shaped, although her fingernails weren't painted. The movements of her fingers in her hair made the silky strands shift and fall back into place. To Callum, the gesture seemed as natural and pretty as a jabiru stretching and folding its glossy wings.

'What would you like for breakfast?' he asked, unhappy to find himself still thinking about her hair, her hands, her feet.

She grimaced. 'I'm not sure. I thought I'd just try a cuppa to start with.'

'You're not hungry?' he challenged.

'Not really. Maybe some dry toast.' She looked away.

He took a deep breath. 'You were sick—just before.'

'It's nothing.'

'Nothing? Are you sure it's nothing, Stella?'

Her head swung back quickly and her grey eyes were defensive as she stared at him. 'Of course I'm sure.'

He knew she was lying.

'I can't let you head off on the long journey back to Sydney if you're not well. And if you can't manage more to eat than dry toast—'

She turned swiftly away from him again. He couldn't be sure but he thought she seemed to be trembling.

'Stella.'

She shook her head as if she wanted him to leave her alone. Then her chin lifted and he saw again the same haughty strength that he'd sensed in her yesterday. Or was it just stubbornness?

When he stepped towards her, she continued to keep her back to him, but he settled his hands firmly on her shoulders and forced her to turn around, too tense to take his time searching for delicate ways to pose his question. 'Stella, are you pregnant?'

'No!' she snapped and she tried to jerk her shoulders out of his grasp. 'Anyway, it—it's none of your business.'

He kept a tight grip on her shoulders. 'If you're carrying my brother's baby, I consider it my business.'

Her eyes blazed with sudden anger. 'Why? What would you want to do about it?'

'Are you telling me it's true?' His breathing felt suddenly constricted. 'You *are* pregnant?'

He let go and she jumped back quickly, like a trapped animal escaping.

'I'm telling you it's got nothing to do with you. I don't want you or your family trying to take over my life just—just because—'

'Just because you're having Scott's baby,' he finished for her. Out of the blue, he felt his eyes sting and his throat close over. Spinning on the heel of his riding boot, he marched away from her, clear across the room, kicking a chair out of his way as he went.

Bloody hell! He mustn't lose it and make a complete fool of himself in front of this woman, but the thought of Scott's seed blossoming inside her made him feel damn emotional.

Scotty Roper was gone for ever, but he'd left behind a part of himself. And, God help him, Callum couldn't block out the thought of his brother and Stella together—making that little baby—making *love*.

Whirling around again, he found that she was close behind him, standing with her hands clasped in front of her, as if she'd been thinking about touching him and hadn't dared, or hadn't wanted to.

'Are you quite certain it's Scott's baby?' he asked coldly.

The way she closed her eyes and compressed her lips told him she hated the question and hated him for asking.

'It's definitely his,' she said, matching his cold tone. 'And if you plan to stand there and make moral judgements about me, I'm going straight out that door and taking off for Cloncurry without even thanking you for your reluctant hospitality.'

'OK. OK.' He raised his hands in a halting action, then let out a long breath. Steam was pouring out of the kettle on the stove and he grabbed the opportunity to change the subject. 'I'll get you that cup of tea.'

In a weird way Stella felt better now Callum knew about the baby. It felt as if at least some of her burden was lifting from her shoulders.

Sharing the news with someone, *even Callum*, after keeping it to herself for so long brought instant relief. But she would have to make him promise not to tell the rest of his family—certainly not his father. Not the Senator!

He handed her a bright red mug and she took a seat at the table. Snatching the chair he'd kicked aside, he turned it back to front and straddled it. Stella tried not to notice the very masculine stretch of his jeans over his strong, muscular thighs. He propped his elbows on the top rung of the chair's ladder back and held his mug in both hands.

She took a sip of tea. It was hot and sweet, just how she needed it. And her stomach seemed to accept it. 'Look,' she said, 'this is my problem, Callum. You don't have to worry about it.'

He eyed her thoughtfully. 'Did Scott know about the baby?'

She shook her head.

'And you came out here to tell him.'

'Yes.'

His brown-gold eyes continued to study her with the

intensity of a hawk. 'What were you hoping? That he would marry you?'

Stella almost dropped her mug. 'No. Not marriage.' Did she imagine that slight relaxation of his shoulders?

'Do you need help? Money?'

'*No!*' She stared at him, shocked. 'And I'm not planning to get rid of it. Is that what you thought?'

He shrugged. 'I'm just trying to understand.'

She wanted to believe him. It was actually a comforting idea—having someone who wanted to understand.

Perhaps he was more sensitive than he appeared on the surface. Perhaps she could trust him. Her chin lifted. 'I know I'll be a hopeless mother, but the least I can do is give this little baby life.'

Draining his tea, he rocked the chair slowly forward and set his empty mug on the table. When he straightened once more, his gaze lifted slowly. 'What makes you think you'd be a hopeless mother?'

She felt her cheeks burn. *She couldn't tell him that.* No way! Honesty had its limits. It would mean confessing about Marlene, her own mother, the source of most of her hang ups. It would mean dredging up those sordid stories about the way Marlene had failed over and over in numerous attempts at motherhood.

It had been the ongoing pattern of Stella's childhood and it left her terrified at the thought of ever attempting to be a mother.

The pattern had always been the same. Marlene would plead with the welfare people that she could take beautiful care of Stella and stay clean and sober. She would promise the earth.

And, because the government policy was to keep mothers and children together wherever possible, they would give in. For a few months, life would be grand. Stella would go home to her mother's new flat and they would eat meat with three kinds of vegetables and they'd go to the movies. They'd play music and dance in the lounge.

Marlene would wash her long black hair and she'd smell of lemon shampoo and talcum powder, and she would take Stella on her lap and read her stories about heroes. For some reason her mother had fancied tales about brave, fearless men.

At night, Marlene would tuck her into bed and tell her she loved her. And Stella would love her back fiercely, so fiercely she could feel her chest swell with the force of her emotion. Marlene was her mother, the very best mother in the world.

But then there would always be the black day when Stella came home from school and found Marlene incoherent and smelling of alcohol. Each day after that things would get worse…the house would turn into a pigsty…and there'd be a different man… She'd go hungry. Sometimes the man would be violent and she'd have to hide outside the house, crying and hungry, trying to sleep in the garage.

Eventually someone, usually a teacher, would report Stella's condition to the authorities. They would take her away again and Marlene would be broken-hearted. She would sob that she wanted to be a good mother…

Stella had wanted her to be a good mother, too. Had longed for it. She'd hated Marlene for failing yet again…

It wasn't the sort of story she could tell, certainly not to this earnest, solemn man, the son of Senator Ian Roper.

'Are you saying you don't want to be a mother?'

I'm terrified. I'm scared I don't know how to be a mother.

'I—I've worked very hard at my career.'

She saw his stony expression and she felt a distinct rush of resentment. It was impossible for anyone else to understand. She cast a frantic glance to the clock on the wall. 'Don't you have to go work or something?'

He rose to his feet slowly and she wished he hadn't. When he looked down at her from his considerable height, she felt smaller than ever.

'I'm waiting to hear from a ringer in Kajabbi,' he said. 'When he's free, we'll take the stock from the holding yards through to the road trains on the highway, but that probably won't happen till tomorrow or the day after.'

He walked to the sink and deposited their mugs into it. 'How about that dry toast?' he asked with a glimmer of a smile.

She had almost forgotten about breakfast. 'Thanks.'

As he dropped two slices of bread into the toaster he turned her way. 'You shouldn't leave this morning. You've barely had time to recover from the long drive up here. You should at least stay another night.'

He wasn't being friendly or warm. Just practical. And the long journey had been exhausting. She hated the thought of heading straight back.

'That would be sensible, I guess. Thanks.'

He brought her dry toast and spread his own with plenty of butter. It melted, warm and golden, into the toasted bread and Stella couldn't help looking at it rather longingly. Her morning sickness was fading and she was feeling hungry again.

'Sure you don't want some mango jam? My sister Ellie makes it.' He spread the bright-coloured fruit onto his toast and took a bite.

'It does look rather good,' she admitted and dipped her knife into the pot.

They munched for some time without talking. Then he said unexpectedly, 'You'd better tell me about this career and these big plans of yours.'

She sent him a hasty, troubled look, then just as quickly looked at her hands clenched in her lap.

'You never know,' he said carefully. 'I might be able to help.'

'How could you?'

'I don't have a damned clue. But if you tell me—'

She shook her head. 'There's no point. No one can help.'

But he wouldn't give up. 'What kind of work do you do? On the one brief occasion we met in the past, I don't think we talked about mundane things like jobs.'

They exchanged one lightning-quick glance, then both looked away. Stella fought to ignore the sudden memory of his strong body, hard against hers, his hot, hard mouth taking hers. 'I—I work with weather.'

'A weather girl? Like on TV?'

'Sort of. I'm not actually on TV, but I help to supply them with their information.'

He frowned. 'You're a meteorologist?'

'Yes.'

'And you couldn't do that if you had a baby?'

'Not—' She took a deep breath. *What the heck? Here goes...* '—not if I was on location in the Orkney Isles or Russia.'

There was no disguising his shock. 'Russia? What kind of job are you talking about?'

She told him about the documentary project scheduled to begin six weeks after her baby was due. 'I'd be based in London, but I'd be expected to travel, mostly studying coastlines. It's a job I've been working towards for ages and an offer like that is highly prized in my circle.'

Callum's lips pursed as he released a low whistle. 'I'll bet it is.'

'But, of course, a newborn baby doesn't fit in the picture.'

He was scowling again. 'I can see how this baby has completely wrecked your plans.' He didn't say anything more for at least a minute, just sat there as if he was carved from stone. At last he said, 'So you didn't want Scott to marry you and you didn't want his money. What was it you wanted from him?'

'It doesn't matter any more. It can't happen.'

'Tell me anyhow.'

Stella ran nervous fingers through her hair. Then she sighed loudly. 'I don't know how to say this without sounding crazy, but I was hoping Scott might be able to look after the baby for a while—so I could still go to London.'

Telling Callum had not been a good idea. He looked pale and distinctly unhappy. He sat staring at the table for several long, silent minutes. At last he spoke very quietly. 'You really are in a bind, aren't you?' And then he ran his big hand over his face, almost as if he was trying to hide his reaction.

Suddenly he jumped to his feet and mumbled that he'd better get on with some work. 'Help yourself to any books or magazines, rest up, watch TV. Eat what you like from the fridge or the pantry.' In the doorway, he turned back. 'I'll leave Mac behind for company.'

Then he hurried down the veranda as if he couldn't wait to get away.

Blackjack's hooves thundered beneath Callum, drumming the hard earth and pounding over the red plains of Birralee. Faster, harder, he pushed his mount, but nothing eased his raging, inner turmoil.

Eventually, he pulled to a shuddering halt on the crest

of a headland that offered spectacular views down a red-walled gorge. It was the place he always came to when he needed to think.

Today his thoughts boiled. Why did it have to be Stella Lassiter who'd come to him with this problem? He didn't know what upset him more: the fact that the woman, who had roused him from apathy to passion in the briefest of encounters, now carried a part of Scott within her and might take it away to the far ends of the earth, or the knowledge that her relationship with Scott had become intimate.

Slumping in the saddle, he sat in a gut-clenched daze while his mind overflowed, teeming with memories of the night he'd met Stella…

He'd gone to Sydney with Scott to check out the prize-winning stock at the Royal Easter Show and, afterwards, Scott had taken him to a party. He'd seen Stella the instant he'd entered the room.

She'd been standing on her own at the far side of the crowd, watching the revellers with her chin at a haughty angle and an aloof expression on her face. Callum had been seized by an urge to stare.

She'd looked bold and bewitching. Her hair had been as dark and shiny as polished ebony and her sleeveless silk dress, the colour of rich claret, vibrant against the smooth ivory of her skin.

Her gaze had met his. She'd looked across at him and had smiled.

And the next moment had been like something out of a movie. He'd begun to walk towards her through the crowd. She'd watched him all the way. When he'd reached her, he'd been strangely out of breath, a little star-struck and suddenly shy, almost embarrassed by the spell that had seemed to have drawn him to her.

But then he'd looked into her clear grey eyes and had felt such a deep, immediate connection that he'd known that if he lived to be two hundred, he would never forget the moment.

Scott's laughing voice had sounded in his ear. 'Oh, so you've met Stella. Good.' He took her hand and placed it in Callum's. 'Stella, this is my big brother, Callum. Be nice to him. He's rough around the edges, but not quite as grim as he looks.'

Then Scott slapped Callum on the shoulder before disappearing off into the crowd to find a drink.

Callum asked Stella to dance and she hesitated at first. Her eyes followed Scott, watching as he reached the bar and started to chat up a pair of pretty girls. In hindsight, Callum realised he should have picked up on the obvious clue of her worried glance after Scott, but he'd been so determined to win her, he'd ignored anything that might get in his way.

When she warmly accepted his invitation to dance, he was as relieved as a nervous schoolboy.

The party's host had hired a band and the music was good. He enjoyed the physicality of dancing. Stella was a responsive partner and the electrifying spell that had drawn him to her continued to weave its sorcery.

Their smiling gazes linked and held as her slender curves brushed against him. He watched the growing warmth and awareness in her eyes as, time and again, their bodies met, tantalised, then swung apart.

When the music slowed, he couldn't wait another heartbeat to draw her closer, but when he did, the slow, sensual swaying of her slim hips beneath his hands and the sweet pressure of her breasts drove him to the limits of his control. He'd never been so highly sensitised, so exquisitely on edge, so jealous of the barriers of thin, teasing silk.

Dancing with Stella, gazing into her eyes, holding her in his arms, inhaling her…wasn't enough.

And the high colour in her cheeks, the wild smoky haze in her eyes and the catch in her breathing told him that she shared the same amazing need that was flaring in him.

He bent his lips to her ear. 'Let's get out of here.'

She nodded quickly and they fled from the brightly lit party rooms into the garden.

Moonlight sheened Stella's hair and silvered her pale skin as he tasted her at last. Her mouth was honey-sweet, yielding and passionate and he kissed her hard, taking everything with no more permission than the promise in her smile.

It was as if Stella was the first woman, the only woman he'd ever kissed, as if her mouth had been fashioned for his mouth and his alone, her breasts for his hands, her sweet femininity for his unforgiving hardness.

God knew what might have happened if the bright laughter of other party guests hadn't sounded close by. Entangled in each other's arms, they stood as quietly as their ragged breathing would allow, while laughing couples wandered past with a clinking of bottles.

When they were alone again, Callum drew her towards him once more, but he knew even before she stiffened and stepped away, that the magic had gone. For her the spell was broken.

'I shouldn't be here,' she moaned. 'We must go inside.'

'Stay,' he ordered, his voice thick and brusque with desire still rampant in his veins.

'I'm not a cattle dog, Callum,' she muttered before turning and walking quickly ahead of him back into the house.

Once inside, she asked for a drink. When he returned with wine, she drank half of it quickly, then placed the glass on a nearby table.

Her hands slid nervously down her thighs. 'Look, what happened out there—I apologise if it looks as if I've been leading you on, but—ah—' She pressed shaking fingers to her chest and shook her head. 'I shouldn't have let you kiss me.' She looked distressed.

He had to clear the tightness in his throat before he could answer. 'I'm not going to apologise for doing something I was sure we both wanted.'

'I'm not blaming you. I know I gave you all the signals. It's—it's just that I shouldn't have—'

His head was still reeling and he grabbed her hand roughly. Too roughly. Leaning close he muttered, 'You're fooling yourself, Stella. You were burning hot.'

'No. No, you don't understand.' She snatched her hand away and looked genuinely frightened. 'I'm sorry, Callum, but I should never have gone outside with you. I'm feeling so guilty.' She dragged in a heavy breath and her grey eyes were dark with confusion. 'You see, I—I already have a boyfriend.'

Just then Scott called to them from across the room. He beamed a cheery grin and waved. The giggling blonde at his side waved as well.

Stella's twisted, sad little smile as she waved back struck Callum like a savage blow. 'Not Scott?' he cried in disbelief. 'You're not trying to tell me my little brother is your boyfriend?'

Her chin lifted and she stared directly at him. For long, painful seconds she looked puzzled and helpless, but then she answered quite definitely, 'Yes, he is.'

He wanted to tell her she was making a huge mistake. There were a thousand reasons why she shouldn't be Scott's girl. Couldn't she see beyond his boyish charm? Didn't she know about his reputation with the ladies? And didn't she understand that she was destined to be with him, Callum?

'I'm very fond of Scott,' she said.

I'm very fond of Scott. Those words had pulled him up sharply as if he'd been snared by a ringer's lasso.

So in the end, the sum total of his relationship with Stella Lassiter had been a few measly hours and a frantic fumble. The brevity of the encounter made a mockery of the strong feelings that still lingered.

He knew he should have been grateful that she had been honest. She'd wanted Scott. Stubborn pride had stopped him from trying to change her mind, from trying to tell her how deeply and sincerely *he* would love her.

He'd left the city and he hadn't gone back.

With a squaring of his shoulders, he watched the flight of a black falcon, wheeling and cruising high above him. Enough of useless rehashing. What he was supposed to be thinking about, what he'd come out here to give deep thought to, was the fatherless baby. Scott's child.

He dug his heels into his horse's flanks and together they took off again at a steady gallop. He owed it to Scott to make sure this child didn't suffer by coming into the world without a father. Oh, yeah. Callum blinked at the sudden stinging in his eyes. He owed Scott big time.

At the far end of the paddock, there was a shallow dam and he led Blackjack there for a drink. Dismounting, he looped the reins over a post and, while the horse took water, he swallowed deep drafts from his water bottle and trickled some of the cool liquid over his hot and dusty face and neck. He rubbed roughly at his eyes.

His father had always joked that boys born in the outback had their tear ducts extracted at birth. They didn't wallow in sentimentality.

But hell! How could he hold back the flood of emotions that came when he remembered his part in Scott's accident? How could he hold back the *guilt?* If only he'd stopped Scott from flying that day. It had been a damn spider bite. One tiny arachnid had caused so much grief.

The morning of the accident, Callum had rolled out of his swag to find a painful welt on his wrist and a redback spider hiding in the depths of his sleeping bag. Although he'd tried to make light of it, he'd felt a little woozy and affected by the poison.

'You're not flying today,' Scott said when he saw Callum's condition. 'You have a spell on the ground with the horses.'

'I'll be fine,' Callum protested. He was a much more experienced pilot than Scott.

'No, mate. Don't try to tough this one out. We don't want you getting dizzy and dropping the chopper. It's a long way to fall.'

If only he'd argued harder! He should have called off the muster for that day. They'd both known that Scott hadn't been experienced enough for the risky flying required in a cattle muster. But his little brother had always loved adventure, and since birth he'd always found a way to get what he'd wanted. That day, he'd wanted to fly.

Callum had been left with an unbearable burden of guilt.

His parents had never openly asked why he'd let Scott fly the chopper, but he'd seen the silent questions in their eyes. They knew that he could have prevented Scott's death and that knowledge ate at him day and night. He'd learned that the one person a man couldn't forgive was himself.

With a heart-rending sigh, he mounted Blackjack again. He'd made the wrong decision that day. Today it was time to make another decision and he knew now with certainty what it must be. If he did nothing else worthwhile in this life, he had to do this. He had to protect Scott's baby.

And if Stella Lassiter wouldn't agree to his plan, he would have to find a way to make her.

CHAPTER FOUR

STELLA wandered about the homestead, unable to concentrate on reading even the lightest book. She kept thinking about Callum's reaction to her confession.

He probably thought she was incredibly selfish, wanting to chase off to London and ditch her responsibilities as a mother. If he hadn't rushed off in such a hurry, she would have explained that she'd already accepted the fact that London was out of the question now.

She drifted with uneasy curiosity from room to room in the Birralee homestead, trying out chairs, looking at family photos, listening to CDs, flicking through magazines...

She even forced herself to think about the letter she must write to the television network. *With deep regret...I am writing to inform...no longer in a position to accept your offer...*

She talked to Oscar and to Mac, but her budgerigar had never been trained to talk and the dog's conversational skills were even more restricted.

In the late afternoon, when she finally heard horse's hooves cantering up the track from the creek, she dashed to a window to look.

Astride a beautiful black stallion, Callum came flying up the slope towards the homestead. Behind him the sun blazed. Stella's breath caught. The man and beast seemed to be riding straight out of the sun like the gods of ancient legends. The sight stirred her. Disturbed her.

Later, when Callum had attended to the horse, he came into the house and she was relieved to see that he looked less like a god and distinctly more human—dusty, sweat-streaked and tired.

'You look like you've put in a hard day's work.'

'A hard day's thinking,' he corrected. Then his eyes narrowed and his intense gaze held hers. 'I'll take a shower and then I'll tell you about it.'

Her mouth dropped open. What on earth did this mean? 'Can't you give me a hint?' she asked his retreating back.

In the hall doorway he paused and looked back over his shoulder. 'I have a proposition to put to you.'

Then he was gone.

She paced the lounge, tense as a guilty schoolgirl summoned to the principal's office. A *proposition?* How could the man disappear for a day, return to drop a bomb like that, and then stroll calmly out of the room to take a shower as if he'd merely mentioned the sky was clouding over?

A proposition? What on earth did he mean? A dozen crazy thoughts chased through her head, but every time she tried to pin one down her mind screwed up with panic.

Pacing the carpet made her feel worse, so she threw herself back into the armchair where she'd spent much of the afternoon with a bowl of dry crackers and a can of lemonade beside her.

Hoping to look much calmer than she felt, she lounged casually in the huge, well cushioned chair with her legs curled beneath her while she flicked through the pages of an out-of-date women's magazine.

At last Callum's footsteps sounded in the hall and she fought the urge to uncurl her legs and to sit straight.

Stay cool. Don't let him think you're worried. After all, a proposition is just a grand word for a suggestion—for advice. You can deal with that. People have been handing out well-meant advice all your life.

When he entered the room, she kept her eyes on the magazine in her lap, flicked another page very slowly and then, just as slowly, allowed her gaze to slide his way.

Big mistake!

Freshly showered, with dark curls still damp, he stood in the middle of the antique oriental carpet and stared down at her. Suddenly her decision to slouch in a chair seemed like a very bad move.

From this position she was forced to look up…and up…to his great height and ridiculously wide shoulders…to his uncompromising jaw and no-nonsense mouth, his excessively brooding brows.

The golden lights in his brown eyes provided the only trace of warmth in his whole face. From this angle, everything else looked huge and grim.

And disturbingly handsome. His lean body, tiger eyes and born-to-be-wild hair carried a mix of danger and beauty that threatened her and yet thrilled her, too.

'Feeling better after the shower?' she asked, determined not to let her confusion show.

'I certainly feel cleaner.' He took a seat in the opposite chair and lounged back.

Stella watched the way he took his time settling his long rangy body into the chair. *He's trying as hard as I am to look calm and together.* The realisation helped to steady her. She picked up a cracker from the bowl beside her and munched it. 'Want one?'

He shook his head. 'We need to talk about your predicament.'

'My predicament?' she repeated slowly. 'I presume you mean my pregnancy?'

'Of course.'

Stay cool! With her legs still curled beneath her, she said, 'I told you not to worry about it, Callum. Good heavens, women have been dealing with this *predicament* since time began.'

'And too many times, they've ended up with the raw end of the deal.'

Bull's eye. That was a hitch she couldn't deny.

Her lips puffed as she let out a long, slow breath. OK, maybe Callum Roper was making a genuine effort to see things from her point of view, but that didn't mean his proposal would be user-friendly.

Reaching sideways, she lifted the bowl from the little table and rested it on her lap, taking her time to select another cracker. 'So what's your grand plan, Callum?'

'It's not so grand. Quite simple really... I'm proposing marriage.'

Her legs shot from under her. Crackers flew over the carpet and she completely forgot to stay cool. *Marriage?* Gripping the arms of her chair, she gaped at him. 'What on earth are you talking about?'

Ignoring the scattered crackers, he said solemnly, 'I see marriage as the best solution to your problem.'

Totally shocked, she struggled for breath. She needed several attempts at breathing before she could speak. 'Are you telling me you want to marry me off to someone?'

He gave the faintest of nods.

'How dare you?' She jumped to her feet. This wasn't something she could take sitting down. 'What right do you have to wreck my life?'

With a face as empty as a blank page, he said calmly, 'Let me finish and I'll explain everything.'

Hands on hips, she glared at him, her breath still shallow and uneven. 'OK,' she said at last. 'Who's the poor sucker you think I should trap into marriage?'

There was a beat of time before he said very simply, 'I am.'

Fresh shock waves sent her sinking back into the chair. Marry *him?* Impossible! A rush of heat engulfed her, bringing with it unwanted memories of that night a year ago when the flames of her desire had been so strong, so animal-like, they'd totally alarmed her.

Her breath came in desperate gasps. 'You're—you're crazy, aren't you?'

'Probably.'

'My God, Callum.' She gave a shaky little laugh. 'Don't joke like that. For half a minute I thought you were serious.'

He didn't move or speak. It was so maddening. He simply lounged lazily in his chair with one riding boot propped casually on the opposite knee. When it came to staying cool, he was winning hands down.

'I am being serious,' he said with an annoying lack of emotion. 'This is a perfectly sensible solution.'

'Sensible? What's sensible about it?' Jumping to her feet again, she flung her hands skywards to emphasise her distress. 'Callum, hello! This is the twenty-first century. Perhaps outback men haven't caught up, but most guys these days understand that women don't appreciate being forced to become a man's possession. That kind of thinking died out in—in the Dark Ages.'

How could he sit there looking so composed? So smug? He had to be crazy.

'No doubt you still think the earth is flat,' she cried.

She couldn't, wouldn't, hang around to listen to this nonsense! Before he could answer, she dashed out of the room and charged down the hallway, not sure where she was running, but needing space to think. To scream?

But the hall led to the front veranda and beyond that there was nothing but endless bush, red-soil plains and kangaroo grass. The outback! With a groan, she sagged against the veranda railing and stared at the darkening bush.

That was all there was out here. Bush, bush and more bush. She'd never realised till now what a luxury it was to have a little coffee shop around the corner from her Sydney flat. Just where did an outback girl go if she needed to have a quiet nervous breakdown?

There was a step behind her and she spun around to find Callum standing in the doorway.

'Are you OK?' he asked softly.

She almost spat another angry retort, but the expression in his eyes stopped her. The blank look was gone and instead she caught a glimpse of vulnerability. She released her own bewilderment in a sigh. 'I guess I'm OK. I can't think. I feel as if you've slugged my brain with a stun gun.'

Slowly he walked across the veranda and leaned against the railing. Too close for comfort. 'I apologise,' he said quietly. 'I guess I made a hash of that.'

His humility surprised her and it was hard to stay mad at him. 'I just don't understand where you're coming from.'

'I—I know marriage isn't the sort of thing you want to think about when you're still in love with my brother.'

She looked away, wondering what he would think if he knew that she'd slipped out of love with Scott with surprising ease once she'd finally accepted how little she'd really meant to him.

Callum cleared his throat. 'I'm not presuming that you'd be my wife in the usual sense. I'm not—I'm not trying to replace Scott. The kind of marriage I'm thinking of would be more of—of a business arrangement than a real marriage.'

Her startled gaze swung back to collide with his. 'What kind of business arrangement?' she whispered.

'Something purely practical so that you could stay here until after the baby's born and then go off to London just as you'd hoped.'

Still go to London? *Clump! Clump!* That was her heart taking off like an overexcited child.

A muscle in his jaw worked. 'Have you given serious thought to what it would be like to leave your baby behind?'

She pressed her fingers against her throbbing temples. Oh, Lord! Her feelings about motherhood were so confused. At times she thought how wonderful it would be to have a little baby of her own, but there were just as many times when she was quite sure that she would be as hopeless at mothering as Marlene had been.

'I have to think about what's best for the baby in the long term. This job could be pivotal to my career. It's something I've been working towards for so long and it will mean earning good money so that I can provide for the baby in the future.'

His expression was thoughtful, so pensive, almost sad, that she felt tears gather in her eyes. She looked away again as she asked in a choked voice, 'What would you plan to do with the baby—when I went away?'

'It would stay here with me. I'd have to get someone in to help of course, but that shouldn't be too hard. I'd make sure it was well looked after.'

'I see. But… Why would *you* want to do that, Callum? And why would you want to go to all the trouble of marrying me?'

An unreadable expression flickered in his eyes. Crossing his arms over his chest, he took his time answering, as if he wanted to get the words right in his head before he spoke. 'Marriage would make the baby legitimate. Part of the Roper clan. I'm afraid that's important to me.'

She nodded. Of course. The family name. 'I can imagine that the son of Senator Ian Roper wouldn't want the embarrassment of an illegitimacy in the family.'

'I want this for Scott's sake. It would mean a part of him could go on living here.'

Then he blinked and turned away sharply, looking out into the darkening bush, and Stella felt that he was seeing things out there in the wide stretch of trees and earth and sky that she could never hope to see, feeling things she would never feel.

'And then when I come back—?'

He looked at her again. 'After London?'

'Yes.'

'You would be free to go.' His Adam's apple jerked in his throat. 'You can get on with your life.'

Free to go. Why did those words make her feel as if a door had been slammed in her face? 'What about the baby?'

'It would stay with me.'

'You mean you want to keep it here? To have it grow up here?'

For long, shattering seconds she waited for his answer.

'Yes,' he said at last. 'That would be part of the bargain.'

A cold, cruel emptiness swept through her. Oh, heavens. She clasped a trembling hand over her stomach. Could she bear to leave her baby behind *for ever*?

'You could see the child whenever you wanted to, of course, but this would be its home. Scott's child should have a chance to grow up in the outback. It's a good life. It builds healthy, independent youngsters.'

'I see.' She clutched at a veranda post for support as her legs turned to water.

She couldn't do it. There was no way she could leave her baby to grow up without her.

Don't be selfish, Stella. Think about what's best for the child. What have you got to offer as a single parent? And you don't have a clue how to be a good mother.

If she agreed to Callum's plan, her baby would grow up as part of the extended Roper family, with grandparents, uncles, aunts and cousins, belonging here on Birralee, loving the bush, just as its father had.

She struggled to keep her mind on practical details. 'So we'd say all the wedding vows about to have and to hold till death us do part, and then what? Would we get a divorce?'

Callum settled back against the railing, and stared at the scuffed toe of his riding boot as he answered. 'That's right. I know it sounds calculated, but I think our motives are justified.'

'You'd be doing it for Scott—for Scott's baby and I'd be doing it for—' Stella gulped. *To give my baby its only chance of a family—a proper family—and to save myself from making a hash of motherhood.* She couldn't admit to that. '—I'd be doing it for my career.'

He nodded grimly.

Surely things couldn't be that simple? There had to be a catch. 'I thought marriage was a rather messy business to undo.'

'I understand it isn't messy if there's never been any—' he swallowed '—any intimacy.'

'Oh?' She looked away and hoped he couldn't see how suddenly hot her cheeks were. 'But you plan for us to live together, as man and wife, until the baby is born?'

'More or less.' He cleared his throat. 'We can keep separate rooms.'

'Yeah, sure.'

He reached over and touched her cheek, just the lightest touch of his leathery finger against her skin, but she jumped. A tremor of pain twisted his mouth momentarily, but he kept his hand at her cheek as he said in a low raspy voice, 'You'd be quite safe, Stella. I won't make the same mistake I made in Sydney.'

'Of course,' she whispered breathlessly.

Then he withdrew his hand. 'My interest in you these days is simply as the mother of my brother's child.'

The remark made her ridiculously angry. 'You see me as an incubator?'

'Aren't you?'

The chauvinist pig! 'I refuse to answer that,' she huffed. 'But you can rest assured, Callum, if I do agree to this, I will *never* contemplate even trying to tempt you.'

'That's good,' he said rather loudly, accompanying his words with a slap of his hand on the timber railing.

'Yes, it's dandy,' she cried.

After another uncomfortable pause, he added, 'Look, this is rather a lot to get your head around. I've had all day to think about it. How about I rustle up some dinner and let you have a bit of space to think to yourself. We don't need to make a decision right now.'

'Sure.' She sniffed and, swinging away from him, she marched to the far end of the veranda where she stood glaring out into the dark lonely bush.

He began to walk back inside.

'Just a minute,' she called after him.

He was right. It *was* too much to get her head around and she didn't want to be left alone on the veranda with so many scary thoughts! 'I've still got too many questions.' Her hands flapped helplessly, echoing her confusion. 'I think I'm going to have to come and pester you. Talk it through.'

He shrugged. 'Whatever you like.'

As she accompanied him back to the kitchen, she clung to one thought: *What I must remember is that my baby would have a family. Not just for a year…but for ever.*

And in the kitchen, her eyes lingered on the mismatched chairs gathered around the big table and the high chair in the corner. Tonight they seemed more charming than ever. She pictured her little baby belonging in this room, a part of the big noisy Roper family, with aunts and uncles and six boisterous cousins.

How many lonely days had she spent as a child wistfully dreaming of a room like this filled with a big rowdy family? She had imagined them all—and in her head they had seemed so real.

Sweet, elderly grandparents who spoiled her; a pretty aunt who bought her brand new books for birthdays and perfume for Christmas; an annoying boy cousin who teased her; a cheery uncle who took time to listen to her dreams—and a father.

Oh, how good and kind her imaginary father had been!

Heavens! How could she bear to give her baby up? But how could she deny it a real chance to have all that?

Callum was rattling around in the pots and pans cupboard. 'Do you like spaghetti?' he called over his shoulder.

'Sure.'

'Good.' He pulled out a huge pot, filled it with water and set it on the stove.

'What can I do to help?'

'You can grate some parmesan cheese. I'm afraid all I'm going to do is heat up a bottle of sauce.'

She managed a smile. 'Now you're talking my kind of cooking.'

He disappeared into the pantry and came back with a packet of spaghetti and a large bottle of Italian-style tomato and garlic sauce.

Grateful for the distraction, Stella hunted down the cheese in the door of the refrigerator, found the grater and a small bowl in a cupboard next to the stove and sat down at the table.

'You know,' she said as she peeled plastic away from the triangle of cheese, 'if we went ahead with this scheme of yours, you'd be getting a pretty poor bargain. I can't cook and I don't know a thing about living in the outback.'

Suddenly the truth of her words hit home. She imagined meeting his family and felt a slam of panic. 'We couldn't do it,' she said quickly. 'It wouldn't work.'

'Why not?'

'Goodness, Callum. There are so many reasons. But number one is I don't fit in here. Look at me.'

'I'm looking. I see one head, two arms, two legs.' His mouth quirked unexpectedly. 'Unusual toenails.'

Suddenly self-conscious, she tucked her feet under the chair. To fill in time during the day, she'd repainted her toenails dark red and had stuck on tiny silver nail ornaments. 'That's what I mean. My toenails are an excellent example of what's wrong about me. My style is completely wrong. I'm a gypsy. I bet the women in your family have little pearl studs in their ears and wear classic country linen shirts with stretch moleskin jeans and are mad about horses…'

'Well…yes.'

'The only horse I've ever ridden was on a merry-go-round. And your mother and sisters are probably brilliant at cooking and sewing. You have a sister who makes jam for heaven's sake. I've never known anyone who didn't just buy it in a jar from the supermarket.'

As if to make up for her lack of skills, she thrust the cheese against the grater with fierce concentration.

'My father's a bit rigid in his ways, but the rest of my family are very easy going really,' Callum said. 'Besides, you won't have to see them very often.'

Not very often would still be too many times, she was sure. But as another dark thought hit, she groaned and the metal grater thumped loudly on the table top.

'What's the problem now?'

'There's an even bigger reason why your people would hate me.'

He stared at her. 'I would never have guessed you were so insecure.'

'Yeah, well, we won't go into that.' Now wasn't the time to confess she was a walking encyclopaedia of insecurities. She began to grate furiously again.

'Hey, we only need a little cheese to sprinkle on top,' he reminded her.

She stopped grating and stared in bewilderment at the ridiculous mountain of shaved parmesan. 'Callum, if we went ahead with this plan, your folks are going to think of me as the trollop who seduced your brother and then found a way to hoodwink you into marriage.'

Slowly, he turned away from the stove and stepped across to the table. His serious gaze held hers as his big hands gripped the back of a chair. 'For the time being,' he said, 'as far as my family are concerned, the baby is mine.'

Stella gasped. His words echoed and tumbled in her head. *The baby is mine.* For a shocking moment, she saw an image of herself and Callum—making love. Her chest seemed to squeeze all the breath from her lungs and an embarrassing coil of heat tightened her insides. *For Pete's sake, get a grip, girl. That's not going to happen.*

As soon as she could speak, she said, 'So you wouldn't tell your family about Scott and me?'

He shook his head. 'I don't think they're ready to deal with that kind of news.'

'You'd be prepared to let them think you and I had some kind of whirlwind romance-cum-shotgun-wedding?'

'Yes. That way we can protect both Scott's reputation and yours.'

'But don't you care what they think of you?'

He looked at the floor for a long, painful moment, was still looking at it as he answered her. 'This way is best. It won't hurt them as much.'

Stella stared at this big, dark, older brother of Scott's and wondered how she'd ever thought he lacked finer feelings. Here he was, calmly offering to sacrifice his reputation and his freedom and not one word of complaint.

'But you'll have to put up with me hanging around your house growing fat. I might drive you nuts.'

'Yeah, you might. I'll just have to cope, won't I?' He moved back to the stove and added sprinkles of dried basil and oregano to the deep red tomato sauce. Then his toffee-brown eyes found hers and he smiled. 'The daily change in toenail colour should keep me entertained.'

Stella knew she blushed. Arguing against his plan was getting harder all the time. She was beginning to feel as if she was in one of those crazy dreams where she'd try to run, but her legs would be made of air; she'd start her car, but the accelerator wouldn't depress; every time she'd try to stand up, she'd fall over.

With his back to her, he dropped long strands of yellow spaghetti into the boiling water. 'We have weather and global warming issues out here, too, you know,' he said without looking her way. 'I'd be the only cattleman in the district with a live-in weather forecaster. You could help me plan the best times to muster, when to bring in feed.'

She had to admit that she always jumped at a chance to apply her scientific knowledge to practical situations.

He must have sensed her interest because, without waiting for her to reply, he went on, 'Every way you look at it, my plan is the best solution.'

Then he turned to her, and the warmth fell out of his face and his mouth tightened with tension as he asked, 'So what do you say, Stella? Taking everything into consideration, will you marry me?'

CHAPTER FIVE

WILL you marry me?

Callum stood stone still, his heart knocking against his ribs. Stella was looking as if she might weep. He couldn't blame her. How rotten could it be to be asked to marry a man under these circumstances?

She'd loved Scott. She was carrying his child. And now, she'd not only lost Scott, but was being asked to give up the child as well.

Was he asking too much?

Was it selfish of him to want to keep his family intact to protect the Roper name? And just how honest was he being with himself? All that high-sounding stuff he'd sprouted. *You'd be quite safe, Stella. I won't make the same mistake I made in Sydney.*

Could he be sure about that? Did he really expect to spend the next few months with this bewitching creature without giving in to all the hot and lusty urges that ravaged him? Was he man enough for the task he'd set himself?

Stella blinked.

Surely she wasn't going to disgrace herself by crying now?

She never cried, so she mustn't start now. She mustn't make this any harder for Callum. How much fun could it be to ask a woman he didn't love—hardly *knew*—to be his wife? She mustn't overload this scene with unnecessary emotion.

She wasn't sure why she felt so choked up. It wasn't as

if she'd spent half her girlhood mooning over dreams about her first proposal. Of course, if she had given it any thought, she might have imagined a rugged, dark and good-looking man like Callum in the picture.

That was beside the point!

The point was the job in London. And providing a family—a *real* family—for her baby.

But marrying Callum Roper? Living out here in the outback alone with him? It was such a scary thought. Scary because she didn't understand her see-sawing feelings for him. The pull of attraction…so thrilling and yet…so threatening.

His face had grown very dark as he waited for her answer. The intensity in his eyes forced her to look away.

'I think your offer of marriage is very generous,' she said quickly. 'But I can't accept.'

He sighed heavily.' You don't have to tell me why. I can guess. I know I'm not Scott.'

'No.'

'I'll never be like Scott.'

She was shocked by the heaviness in his voice. 'I don't expect you to be like him.'

He grunted something she couldn't make out.

Jumping to her feet, she began to circle the table. 'This marriage scheme can't be my only option!'

'Can you think of another solution?'

'I'm working on it.'

'Where else could you stay that's out of the way, where you can keep your pregnancy under wraps?'

'I—I'm sure I'd find another job for the next few months—something—somewhere.'

'And then when you leave, who would look after your baby? Scott's baby?'

She stopped pacing. 'I'd find someone.'

'You have family?'

'No.'

'None at all?'

'I'm afraid not. But—' Shaking her head, she stared at him helplessly. Oh, Lord. Once again she'd run full circle and was back at the same painful place. 'Your plan really is the best, isn't it?'

'No doubt about it.' His mouth thinned and he looked embarrassed. 'Look, I said it before, but I swear it. I won't make any—ah—marital demands.'

'Yes. Yes, I realise that.' Why did he have to make such a federal case of explaining that he'd lost interest in seducing her?

'And maybe in the future, after you've finished in England, we could come to some kind of fair deal about sharing access to the baby.'

'That—that would be good.'

'So?'

So she'd run out of objections.

When Callum's sisters had been married, their weddings had been at Birralee, with guests flying in from all over the country and caterers travelling the long journey from Mount Isa.

For Callum and Stella, things were different. As soon as Callum had moved the cattle to the road trains, they drove into Cloncurry to be married by an obliging, elderly minister who didn't ask too many questions.

Callum took the Range Rover, which at least provided air-conditioned comfort, but for much of the way, they rattled and bumped over a rough, red dirt track.

Beyond Kajabbi, they turned onto the main road, a thin strip of blue bitumen bordered by more red dirt which was, in turn, edged by grass the colour of pale champagne.

Beyond the grass, wattle dotted the wide, terracotta plains in soft green and gold clumps, and above the whole brightly coloured land arched an enormous, very blue and cloudless sky.

Beside him, Stella sat without talking. She was dressed in a long white shirt over white wide-leg trousers. Every so often he glanced her way, but she seemed to be in a pensive mood and he could think of nothing really appropriate to say.

She didn't look as if she was in the mood for jokes, or small talk, or any kind of talk, for that matter.

She looked…lovely. Her clothes couldn't be simpler, but she'd done something fancy with her hair. Bits of it were gathered on top of her head and other bits hung in black silken strands around her face. It should have looked messy, but Callum thought it made her look especially glamorous.

He had donned a charcoal-grey suit, a brand new white shirt and a silver and charcoal striped tie. The mirror told him he'd pass muster as a bridegroom, but he preferred clothes with a lived-in look and feel.

Today he felt citified, spruced up and starchy.

And nervous.

Stella's silence made him nervous.

He knew that one reason she avoided talking was because she was still suffering from morning sickness and he drove as carefully as he could to avoid jolting her more than was necessary. But he was the first to admit he knew very little about what women wanted, and he worried that today she was having regrets about her wedding—about how this day should have been.

No doubt she'd hoped for the whole traditional, romantic bit, the full rhapsody. A proposal of undying love from a man on his knees…a wedding gown and veil…church bells and a choir…family and friends…

One thing was damn sure.

She would have preferred to be marrying his brother, the man she'd loved. The father of her child.

But there was absolutely nothing he could do about that.

He didn't let his mind linger too long on his own reasons for proposing this marriage. That was a dead-end track. It always started with telling himself that he genuinely liked the idea of having a child to raise. He would have had one or two of his own by now if he'd found the right woman.

But when his thinking reached that point, his mind stuck like a needle in a broken record. The right woman. The right woman. After that he couldn't get past the idea of Stella in his arms and her sweet, passionate mouth surrendering to him…

When they reached Cloncurry, he didn't drive straight to the church. He pulled up outside a store managed by a hairdresser, who also doubled as the outback town's florist.

'Why are we stopping here?'

'I won't be a tick,' he reassured her.

Sandy, the shop's owner, grinned when she saw him. 'Wacky-do, Callum. Don't you scrub up a treat!'

A young girl, who was washing a customer's hair at a basin, stared his way and let out a low whistle. 'You look truly dudesome, man.'

'Were you able to get what I ordered?' he asked Sandy.

'I did my best. What do you think of these? They came in from Mount Isa only half an hour ago.'

She reached behind a partition and with an enormously bright smile, brought forth a pretty arrangement of white roses, carnations and baby's breath tied together with a broad white satin ribbon.

'They're terrific, Sandy,' he said and, as she handed them to him, he caught their heady, sweet fragrance. *This should help to make her feel a little more like a bride.* 'Thanks.'

Outside again, he leapt back into the driver's seat and handed the bouquet to Stella. For some ridiculous reason his hands were shaking and he could swear hers were, too, as she accepted it.

'Thank you,' she whispered. Her eyes glowed and she dipped her face towards the delicate blooms, breathing in their perfume. The movement sent fine strands of her hair falling forward, sweeping over her soft cheek. He'd never seen anything so captivating.

'Wouldn't seem like a wedding without flowers,' he said.

'No.'

He could sense her tension as he drove two streets further on to the little wooden church. Of course, he didn't blame her for feeling so edgy. He was as strung out as fencing wire.

There were no other cars parked outside when they pulled up, but that was what he expected. He and Stella had agreed that the wedding should be as quiet as possible. No family or friends. No fuss. Just get the papers signed and then get back to Birralee.

'But if you don't mind,' Stella had said, 'I'd like to wear white. I know it's supposed to be for virgins and all that, but—' she'd compressed her lips for a second or two, before flashing him a brave smile and saying '—this might be the only time I get married, so I'd like to look vaguely bridal.'

It had been then that Callum had decided to get the flowers and it had been since then that he'd found himself more and more worried about how desperately sad this day might be for her.

The day she should have married Scott.

As he turned off the ignition, he warned her, 'Being a bride means you have to let a fellow open the car door for you.'

'OK.'

He hurried to her side of the vehicle, opened the door and held out a hand to help her. She looked at him. Her face was pale above the white flowers but her grey eyes shone softly. 'Thank you.'

In one graceful movement, she left the car and was standing beside him in her simple loose white shirt and trousers, holding the flowers in both hands, close to her heart. 'Scott was the first man who ever opened a car door for me and you're the first man who's ever bought me flowers.'

Callum shrugged. 'You can't beat old-fashioned country boys.' Only just in time, he stopped himself from telling her that she was the first woman he'd ever bought flowers for. Buying flowers, making a fuss over a woman, wasn't his usual style.

Lifting her face to his, she kissed him suddenly. A quick, soft kiss, that lingered fragrant and warm just to one side of his mouth and sent him reeling into the church as dizzy as a drunken sailor.

The wedding wasn't quite the ordeal Stella had feared. She had planned to endure the ceremony bravely, getting through it by thinking of the excitement of going to London.

But she hadn't been prepared for the quaint appeal of the old wooden church with its sweet-faced, elderly minister, or the enthusiasm of his two middle-aged daughters,

dressed in their best pastel frocks, who served enthusias-
tically as witnesses, wedding guests and choir.

One of the daughters cried, actually *cried*, when her father told Callum and Stella, 'I now pronounce you husband
and wife.'

And when it seemed that her father had forgotten an
important instruction, the other sister eagerly prompted
Callum, 'You can kiss the bride.'

And Callum, apparently unwilling to disappoint them,
took both Stella's hands in his and drew her close and then
closer until his arms enfolded her.

'Let's keep up appearances,' he whispered against her
ear.

She felt her face flame at the very thought of exchanging
a kiss with him now, in front of witnesses. But before she
could say anything, he had already started! His mouth was
against hers, touching her politely, almost shyly, with only
the subtlest of pressure.

Relieved to discover how easy he was making this for
her, she kissed him back, returning the warm pressure. In
contrast to the hard, muscled strength of his body, his lips
felt surprisingly gentle and sensitive and...seductive.

But when she expected the kiss to end, his hands continued to hold her close. His warm breath mingled with
hers and his lips brushed her mouth again, as if they were
reluctant to leave her, and her blood hummed through her
veins urging her to stay close to this sweetest of sensations.

And suddenly he was kissing her again and this time
there was nothing, absolutely nothing chaste or proper
about Callum's kiss. No longer was he simply going
through the motions.

His mouth was demanding intimacy. She felt both shock
and pleasure at his daring and her mind and body melted
as the long lingering kiss drove everything else away.

She stopped thinking about the Reverend Shaw and his daughters, stopped reminding herself that this was a charade, even stopped thinking about the last time he'd kissed her. She focused completely on now and this kiss…

His powerful arms tugged her harder against him and he slipped his tongue boldly into her mouth, and he felt so right inside her, so necessary, that she felt herself dissolving into a helpless puddle of pleasure.

She heard one of the sisters sigh. 'Now, that's what I call a kiss.'

At last, too soon, Callum released her and she avoided touching a hand to her surprised lips or looking his way. It would be too embarrassing if he read in her eyes how incredibly affected she'd been. *Again.*

And she didn't want to see how he was feeling. He would be as aware as she was that this kiss hadn't been strictly in line with their plans.

To her dismay, she felt so overcome that she swayed on her feet.

'Are you all right?' Callum asked.

'Just a little dizzy.'

The Reverend Shaw and the Misses Shaw looked concerned.

Callum placed a steadying arm around her shoulders and she took a deep breath.

'Thanks, Callum,' she murmured. 'I'll be fine.'

'Take it easy,' he whispered, drawing her head onto his shoulder. 'Do you want to sit down?'

She shook her head and shortly afterwards the dizziness passed. They collected their marriage certificate and left, but the memory of that kiss lingered as they had a cup of tea in a Cloncurry café, made a quick round of the supermarket to stock up on stores, then drove back to Birralee.

It was so strange to come back to the homestead as husband and wife. Strange because nothing was different.

Callum disappeared almost as soon as he'd parked the Range Rover. Stella went into the kitchen, stacked the groceries away in the pantry and then changed from her white clothes into her everyday black jeans and dark red shirt.

She put her bridal bouquet into a crystal vase and set it on the antique sideboard in the lounge. It looked elegant and suitably old-fashioned, very at home amidst the mellow tones of rosewood and cedar furniture. But she felt more alien than ever—a complete outsider.

She'd been so keyed up about the wedding and now she felt as flat as the snake they'd seen run over by a road train on the highway. She was tired from her morning's ordeal, but not tired enough to sleep. Just weary enough to be moody. Depressed and lonely. Rattling around in this big empty house in the middle of nowhere with nothing to do but change Oscar's food and water and paint her toenails.

But she'd painted them yesterday—a pretty pearly silver. It had been the closest she could get to something bridal. Why had she bothered? She'd been a bride for five minutes.

And now she was simply a wife.

In name only.

Her hands wandered to her lips. Callum's kiss had been so different from the last time he'd kissed her. So sensitive at first, so sweet. So seductive. *But just as risky!*

Ye gods, all she could think about was wanting more. She was like a weak-willed moth drawn to his powerful flame. But just like the moth, she would be burned if she wasn't very careful. The kind of passion Callum could awake in her was too dangerous.

She needed to stay in complete control of her feelings…and her future.

After dinner, they sat on Birralee's front steps with Mac safely between them. Callum drank coffee and Stella sipped peppermint tea while they watched the full moon rise above the cliffs on the far side of the creek.

It started as a silvery glow lighting the sky above the cliff tops and silhouetting the rocky outcrops, making them jet black against an iridescent grey sky.

As they watched, Callum asked unexpectedly, 'So your middle name is Catalina?'

Stella shrugged. 'It's funny the things you find out when you get married, isn't it, Callum *Angus* Roper?'

He grinned. 'Angus is an old family name. It's been hanging around the Ropers for generations. What about Catalina? It sounds Spanish. Do you know where it comes from?'

'Ah…' Stella's mind raced. She didn't have a clue why her mother had selected her names. It hadn't been something she'd got around to discussing with Marlene. 'My mother found Catalina in a book and took a fancy to it.'

He accepted this invention with a slight nod. 'I suppose it's too early to start thinking about what you might call your baby.'

Startled, she stared at him. This afternoon she'd actually forced herself to look at websites dealing with pregnancy and childbirth and she'd ordered some books over the internet, but she hadn't given a moment's thought to baby names. It was easier to think about going away if she thought of the baby as an 'it', an embryonic entity—not a potential little boy or girl. Someone with a name.

She shook her head. 'I don't think I'll be pushing to call it Angus or Catalina.' And then, because she didn't want him to think she was hopelessly unmotherly, she said quickly, 'I think I'll call it Ruby if it's a girl.'

'Ruby,' he repeated slowly. 'Ruby Roper.'

'Look,' she said, jumping to her feet and needing to distract him from coming up with a string of names that were an improvement on Ruby. 'Here comes the moon.'

She pointed to the eyebrow of bright light glistening whitely above the cliff top. 'Watching the moon rise is very different from a sunrise, isn't it?'

'As different as night and day,' he said dryly.

But Stella ignored his sarcasm. She was determined to make a point—any point that had nothing to do with baby names. 'Even primitive people who didn't know anything about science could see for themselves how distinctly different the moon and the sun are. Look!'

In silence they watched the grandeur of the full moon rising like a dignified queen until its complete silver disc emerged above the cliff and sent shimmering light pooling over the bush.

'The moon is mysterious and magic,' she said, 'but the sun is bold and showy.'

'I guess so.'

'I'm sure that's why ancient people decided that the moon is female and the sun is male.'

'You're probably right,' he said, warming to the change of subject. 'And these days there's a new theory about women coming from Venus and men from Mars.'

Stella rolled her eyes. 'Now, I can't accept *that*. Men like to argue that there's a huge difference between the sexes, because it helps to keep women in their place.'

'So you don't think there are fundamental differences between males and females?'

'Well...no,' she hedged cautiously. This wasn't at all what she wanted to be discussing. 'If I'd listened to that kind of talk, I'd never have had the courage to study a male-dominated subject like physics.'

Suddenly he reached down, picked up her hand and placed it on top of his. In the moonlight, she saw how excessively white and slim her hand looked as it lay against the hugeness and darkness of his. The slim gold band he had placed on her fourth finger glowed. Ever so briefly, he touched the ring with one finger.

Stella's heart did a drum roll. Lord help her! How would she cope with this electric tension every time Callum touched her?

He flipped their hands over, palms up, showing the rough, callused pads of his fingers and the soft city-smoothness of hers.

She heard his low chuckle.

'You're right. There's absolutely no difference between a man and a woman whatsoever.'

Then he suddenly jerked his hand away from hers as if he'd realised just how much of a mistake it was for him to be touching her.

Stella felt instantly abandoned and miserable. She had been trying to forget that this was their wedding night, trying not to think of what would have happened if they'd been any other married couple. 'I'm incredibly tired,' she muttered and forced a loud yawn.

Stooping to pick up the empty mugs, she didn't look at him. 'I think I'll hit the hay.' And, feeling more miserable than ever, she hurried away so quickly she barely heard his 'Goodnight.'

Long after Stella had left, Callum sat on the steps with only Mac for company. At first he concentrated on the sounds of the bush at night. The whispering rush of a breeze as it rippled through the tree tops, the occasional low bellow from cattle down near the creek, the distant karoar, karoar, karoar of a lonely curlew.

Stella's deep, smoky, sexy voice.

He couldn't get enough of that voice.

Damn it! He was doing it again. Unless he kept his mind strictly under control he found himself thinking about her—thinking in ways that would lead him to trouble.

Sitting with his elbows propped on his knees, he gripped his head in his hands. This had to stop!

He was intensely aroused by everything about Stella: her sultry voice, her silky hair, the way she moved like a proud princess, the fact that she tasted of heaven when he kissed her.

'I was a prize idiot to kiss her like that,' he muttered to the dog at his side.

How had he ever thought he could have this woman living under his roof for months on end without falling under her spell?

The only, only thing that would keep him from breaking his own crazy rules would be remembering that she'd been Scott's woman. She was carrying Scott's child. And she would be leaving as soon as it was born.

CHAPTER SIX

MORNINGS on Birralee began with a screech of galahs. The pink and grey parrots, which looked ten times prettier than they sounded, took off from the trees along the creek at the crack of dawn. Shortly after that, Stella heard Callum moving about the house.

When she came into the kitchen, he was already tucking into bacon and eggs.

'How's the morning sickness?' he asked as she helped herself to a bowl of muesli and took a seat at the table.

'Seems to be calming down at last.' After a mouthful of food she added, 'I want to find ways of making myself useful around the place.'

His eyes widened over the rim of his big mug of tea. 'That spread-sheeting software you installed on my computer last week is exceptionally useful.'

'I like doing that sort of thing, but if I'm going to be here till the baby arrives, I should face up to some of the things I don't like.'

'You want to help me spey some cows?'

'Good grief, no.' She pulled a grimace of mock horror. 'I don't know if I could ever do that to a cow. Well, not unless she had counselling first.'

Callum laughed.

She grinned back at him. 'Perhaps I should develop a whole new career path for myself as a family planning consultant for cows.'

His smile faded. 'You're missing your work, aren't you?'

'I guess so,' she said as she reached for the milk jug. 'But I think what's bugging me most is that I don't feel I can contribute to anything here. At least I should be doing something about my deficiencies in the kitchen.'

'You're pretty good at washing-up.'

She shot him a give-it-a-miss scowl. 'You know I'm talking about cooking.'

Pushing his empty plate aside, he selected an orange from the fruit bowl and peeled its skin away from the flesh with long deft fingers. With a slow smile, he said, 'But, for a bright girl like you, cooking should be a breeze.'

'Well, it's not.'

His lazy smile lingered. 'I thought all women knew how to cook.'

'Shows you don't know much about women.'

'About city women,' he corrected.

'You know nothing about *this* city woman.' She sniffed and the friendly morning atmosphere was suddenly tense and strained. Closing her eyes, Stella took a deep breath. 'Sorry. It's a sore point. I'm afraid I know as much about cooking as I do about brain surgery or—or black magic.'

He chewed an orange segment thoughtfully. 'Perhaps you could look at cooking as a scientific experiment.'

'Oh, yeah?'

'Sure. Think about it. Cooking is simply a process whereby certain chemicals are combined. There are reactions and if you apply heat there are new reactions. If you vary the chemicals or vary the heat you get different results.'

She stared at him. 'For half a minute you almost convinced me.'

'But it's true!'

'Nice try, Callum, but I happen to know that cooking is a mysterious secret handed down from mothers to their daughters.' She pointed her spoon at him. 'Or occasionally their sons.'

He continued to eat his orange without offering a response.

'All my friends seem to have special secret family recipes. My flatmate, Lucy, could be tortured before she'd hand over her mother's recipe for cherry-ripe slice.'

'Doesn't your family have any cooking secrets?' he asked.

'No,' she answered sharply.

He looked at her for a long moment, as if waiting for her to say more, but she still wasn't ready to confess about her non-existent family. After a minute or two, he rose from the table and crossed to the old pine dresser that stood against the far wall.

Intrigued, Stella watched as he opened one of its drawers, extracted an old exercise book and brought it back to her.

'This is my grandmother's recipe book,' he said. 'It's rather old-fashioned, but she kept all her favourite recipes in here. And my mother's added to it as well. Why don't you take a look?'

'No one will mind?'

'Of course not.'

She stared at the tattered old book. In copperplate handwriting on the front cover was the name Eileen Roper and then, underneath it, Margaret Roper.

Eileen Roper...Margaret Roper...the wives of Roper men...

Stella Roper... Her spine tingled. OK, the other women were proper wives, but maybe, for just a little while, she could pretend she was really a part of this family...a link in the long chain of Roper women who had cooked in this lovely old kitchen.

Feeling like an intruder, she opened the bulging book. The very first recipe was for a rich fruit cake with a note in Eileen's handwriting saying, 'Keeps well and is excellent for the boys to take on a muster'.

Wow! Stella knew her friends would laugh if they could see how excited she was, but for her the idea of making a traditional home-made fruit cake seemed magical. The kind of thing *other* people did! She turned more yellowing pages. There were all kinds of recipes… 'Eileen's chicken and barley soup, good for patients with 'flu…Margaret's caramel rum pie, Angus's favourite…Ellie's beef strog…'

They weren't entered in any particular order and sometimes there was different handwriting as if friends had also written their recipes into the book.

Stella was fascinated. 'Thanks, Callum. I wonder if I should try some of these?'

'Sure. Feel free.'

She flipped back to the first recipe at the front of his grandmother's book. The fruit cake. What a buzz she'd get from making something like that. Perhaps Callum was right. Maybe it was purely a matter of science. If she followed Eileen's instructions to the letter, this scary collection of ingredients could emerge as a real cake.

She forced herself to think positively, imagining herself handing around slices of rich, fruity cake to members of Callum's family.

This is delicious, Stella. Did you make it yourself?

It tastes just like Mother's old recipe.

How could anyone be frightened of a fruit cake? All she had to do was throw fruit, butter, eggs and flour together. She ran her eye down the list of other ingredients Eileen had penned—lemon rind, golden syrup, marmalade, mixed spice, cinnamon and rum.

Already she could imagine this kitchen filling with the enticing smells of citrus and spice. 'I'm going to do this!'

'Do what?'

'Make a fruit cake.'

His eyebrows rose. 'I guess it doesn't hurt to aim high.'

She felt a stab of disappointment. 'You think I should start with something simpler?'

After only a moment's hesitation, he said, 'No. Not at all. You cook whatever takes your fancy.' He pointed to the set of keys hanging on the hook near the door. 'You'll need that big black key. It's the key to the storeroom. You should find everything you want there.'

'I'll have a beautiful big bowl of chopped raisins, cherries and dates soaking in rum for you to admire when you come home tonight, Callum. Prepare to be impressed.'

She smiled up at him, but wished she hadn't. There was a strangely ambiguous expression in his eyes, as if he didn't know whether to smile back or to scowl, and the very uncertainty in his look sent icy shivers skittering down her arms.

'I'll look forward to this evening,' he said quietly, and in one flowing movement he swept his hat from its peg and was out the door, leaving the fly-screen to swing shut behind him.

At noon the following day, Callum and two men from a neighbouring property were busy repairing the holding yard fences and they didn't hear the motor vehicle approach.

Callum was working with a chain-saw and it screamed and whirred shrilly. Sweat gathered beneath his hat and ran in rivulets down his back, making his cotton shirt cling to his skin. Sawdust coated his sweat-dampened arms.

A few metres away, Jim Walker, an aboriginal stockman, bent over a post-hole digger that shuddered and roared as loudly as Callum's chain-saw and, nearby, Jim's brother, Ernie, wielded an axe as he cut a mortise into a bloodwood post.

It was only when Callum caught a flash of white dancing at the edge of his vision that he looked up and was startled to see Stella.

Looking fresh and clean and heart-stoppingly pretty in a snowy white shirt and blue gypsy skirt, she was hovering some distance away, clutching a cane basket against her chest as if she was trying to keep its contents free of saw-dust.

What on earth was she doing here?

He switched off the saw and waved and she called something back, but he couldn't hear her over the noise of the post-hole digger.

'Everything OK?' he yelled.

She nodded. She certainly didn't look as if she'd dashed down here in an emergency. But surely this wasn't a social visit? Wiping his grimy face with his sleeve, he set the chain-saw aside and hurried towards her.

A glance over his shoulder towards the other men assured him that their concentration was still firmly fixed on their work. They were tackling a big job and they needed to finish it today.

'Did you want something?' he asked when he reached her.

She looked embarrassed and made a little gesture with the basket. 'I—I brought you some lunch.'

'Lunch?' His jaw dropped so quickly it was a wonder it didn't hit the hard ground.

'Do you stop for lunch?' she asked.

'Well, yes, we do.'

'I wasn't sure. With all my sleeping in over the past

weeks and everything, I've never noticed if you take lunch with you. I didn't know if you cut sandwiches, or what you do and—and—' she glanced towards Ernie and Jim '—I—I didn't know you had other men working with you.'

Suddenly the noise behind him stopped. Callum looked back to see the Walker brothers' big, white-teethed grins. 'These blokes have come over from Drayton Downs for the day to give me a hand with the fencing repairs.' He beckoned to them. 'Ernie, Jim, come and meet Stella.'

They continued to grin shyly as they ambled over and shook her hand. 'Pleased to meet you, Mrs Roper.'

'Mrs Roper?' Callum frowned at them. 'How did you blokes know I was married?'

They grinned some more and nodded. 'The boss was in Cloncurry yesterday. Word's spreadin' fast that you got yourself hitched, Callum.'

'Why didn't you say something before this?'

'We figured—maybe you was—' Jim shrugged '—maybe it was secret business.'

Stella fiddled with the blue and white tea towel that covered the contents of her basket.

'So what have you got there?' Callum asked her.

'Just—just a salad.'

He picked up a corner of the tea towel and saw two bowls lined with lettuce leaves and filled with dainty spoonfuls of tinned tuna and baby corn spears, cherry tomatoes and cubes of cheese. 'That—that looks great!' He hoped his enthusiasm didn't sound forced.

'I'm afraid I didn't bring enough for everyone.'

'No worries. There's plenty of tucker here for the boys.' He shrugged in the direction of the Esky sitting in the shade of a gidgee bush. He'd packed it that morning with a loaf of bread, a generous hunk of corned beef, a jar of pickles and half a dozen cold boiled potatoes—enough for three hungry men.

Stella's chin lifted and her grey eyes flashed. Hell, she looked sexy when she went into haughty mode. If he wasn't so dirty, dusty and sweaty... If these two grinning blokes weren't gaping at them... If...

Dream on, mate. You're never going to do anything with this bewitching wife...except maybe eat her elegant lunch.

'You don't have to eat this, Callum. I just got carried away with being domesticated this morning.' There was a sudden gleam of triumph in her eyes as she added, 'The fruit cake's in the oven and it smells wonderful.'

'That's terrific.'

Her excitement about cooking was puzzling. Last night, she'd been bursting with pride as she'd asked him to admire the huge bowl of dried fruit she'd spent all afternoon chopping so she could soak it overnight in rum and sherry.

She was getting such a kick out of baking this cake. And yet, a few days earlier, she'd mentioned ever so casually that last summer she'd flown in a Hurricane Hunter jet while tracking a cyclone. They'd gone right into the eye of a storm. Now *that* was something to get excited about.

'The cake takes four hours to bake,' Stella said. 'So I thought I'd have plenty of time for a—' She looked around at the dry, dusty stock yards and pulled a rueful smile. 'I guess there's nowhere to have a picnic here.'

'We can manage a picnic,' he reassured her. 'Hop back in the ute and we'll go down to the creek.'

He did his best to ignore the chuckles of the two brothers as he followed Stella to the ute. Halfway across the yard, she turned back. 'I don't suppose we can avoid having people in the district know we're married.'

'Not much chance,' he agreed. 'Actually, I suppose I

should have warned you. I rang my parents' place in Canberra, but there was no one home, so I left a message on their answering machine. But once they know, the whole world will know about us.'

She took a deep breath as if mentally preparing herself for the fateful day when she would have to face his family, then walked ahead of him again, keeping her head high and her shoulders very straight.

Callum found himself watching the silky sway of her hair and the gentle curve of her bottom beneath her soft cotton skirt and he hoped he'd get through this picnic of hers without making a fool of himself.

This wasn't a good idea.

Even before they reached the creek, Stella regretted her impulse to bring Callum a picnic lunch. The shock on his face when she'd arrived at the yards had been bad enough, but then she saw the poorly disguised smirks of the stockmen and Callum's polite but unenthusiastic reaction to the food she'd prepared and, suddenly, everything felt wrong.

She wanted to tell him she'd changed her mind. He should go back to Ernie and Jim. But he was starting up the ute, accelerating forward…and if she sent him back now, he'd lose face in front of the men.

By the time he parked the ute at the top of the creek bank, her stomach was tight with tension. When he led her to a soft grassy shelf on the lower bank, her mouth went dry.

'This is a good spot for a picnic,' he said, pointing to the shade cast by an enormous paperbark tree, but all she could see was a picture of the two of them sitting there…alone…and she knew a picnic was the most brainless idea she'd ever hatched.

The setting was faultless. Beside them, the cool clear

creek bubbled charmingly over smooth water-washed stones. Blue dragonflies hovered and darted over the water, and a handsome kingfisher gave smooth presentations of precision diving. Yes, everything was perfect.

Not that Stella noticed once Callum crouched beside the creek and hauled off his shirt. She took one look at his wide, bronzed shoulders tapering down to a taut, lean waist and forgot how to breathe.

He began to wash away the sawdust and grime, evidence of his morning's work. Sloshing the water over his back, he let it run in a glistening cascade over his tanned skin and satiny muscles. Her palms grew hot with the thought of touching him, of learning the texture of that strong, smooth back, of feeling those muscles flex beneath her hands.

He stood and turned and she saw his broad, hairy chest and the teasing trail of dark hair disappearing into his jeans...

She shouldn't stare...

But what else, in heaven's name, could a girl do? Callum was truly breathtaking.

Unlike Scott, who'd worn his sex appeal like an advertisement, Callum moved with the natural, unaffected ease of a wild creature. He seemed to live in his body as if he were completely unaware of its charms. As he walked up the bank towards her, did he have any idea he was scrambling her brain?

Perhaps he did and took pity on her. With an easy shrug of his shoulders, he pulled the shirt back on, but when he reached her she was still completely tongue-tied. She handed him his lunch and neither of them seemed to have any idea what to say.

She kicked off her shoes and curled her feet beneath her, but her appetite had deserted her. Callum sat with his knees bent, staring at the creek and forking his lunch into his mouth so quickly she was sure he would get indigestion.

'You're repairing fences?' she asked. Dumb question, but they had to talk, had to find some way to relax and get over this silly awkwardness.

Still chewing, he grunted in agreement.

She tried another desperate tack. 'Have Jim and Ernie lived in this district long?'

He nodded and swallowed. 'All their lives. Their people are Kalkadoons.'

Kalkadoons! An exchange of information at last. 'The Kalkadoons were a very fierce aboriginal tribe in the old days, weren't they?'

He nodded.

'Ernie and Jim seem so shy and friendly.' She waited uneasily for Callum to comment, but he seemed to have forgotten that the art of conversation was a two-way process.

Embarrassed, she dumped her food back in the basket and jumped to her feet. Sitting there on the velvety grass beside him was completely wrong. Dangerously wrong. She should never have suggested a picnic. They were too close, too alone, too awkward with each other...

Picnics were for courting couples.

Grabbing her skirt around her, she stepped down into the creek and dabbled her bare feet in the clear stream, hoping its coolness would reduce the heat racing through her.

'Stella, that isn't a good idea.'

The warning in his voice startled her. Clutching her skirt even higher, she hurried back towards the bank. 'Are there crocodiles here?'

'No!' A fleeting grin quirked his mouth, but next minute

his face grew dark and he stared at her feet. 'You keep flaunting those naked feet in front of me and we'll both be sorry.' His voice held the hint of a growl.

Naked feet? She looked down and caught a glimpse of white toes, blue nail polish and her favourite ankle chain, then she lifted her eyes to Callum and seconds ticked by as she stood there with water swirling around her ankles, her gaze caught in his smouldering glare.

It was happening all over again. That spectacular rush of awareness that had drawn them together in Sydney. Hapless moths hurling themselves towards flames.

In one seamless movement he rose to his feet. 'I've finished my lunch. I should get back to work.'

'Of course.' She scrambled back out of the water and slipped her damp feet into her shoes. 'Let's go, then,' she said, knowing he was wise to leave. Now. They had no chance of a relaxing picnic.

Halfway up the bank, he turned and offered her his hand, muttering, 'This bit's pretty steep.'

Stella looked at his big brown hand and felt ridiculously self-conscious. And, when she placed her hand in his, electric shivers travelled under her skin.

He pulled her to the top of the bank so effortlessly that she stumbled against him and her breasts, tender from her pregnancy, collided with the solid musculature of his arm. An involuntary 'Ouch' escaped.

'What is it?' he whispered and he took half a step back, his eyes dark with emotion. And his gaze continued to hold hers as his hand skimmed the newly lush swell of her breast. He cupped its shape through the soft cotton of her shirt and she heard her heartbeats pounding in her ears as very slowly, very gently, his thumb glanced across the tip.

Oh, Callum. Oh, help! Melting, languorous yearning

flowed through her and she blushed as she felt her nipples hardening and peaking.

'Are they tender?' he asked.

'Just a little,' she whispered.

For too long they stood together with his hand cupping her, heartbeats away from more touching. She could read the tortured questions in his eyes. Knew he was on the brink of breaking down every barrier he'd carefully erected. Understood that he was seeking painful answers in her eyes.

And all she knew was that she wanted him to caress her more boldly. To make the heat that was threading her veins blaze out of control.

But, with a sharp hiss of in-drawn breath, he dropped his hand to his side and stepped away. 'Best get back to work,' he said thickly.

Her breath rushed out in a noisy sigh. The danger was over. She knew she should be grateful that her inner weaknesses hadn't been exposed…but she wasn't grateful at all.

They turned and walked back to the ute.

Back in the kitchen, she knew she should never have left it. Dumping the basket on the table, she let out another long sigh. How had she ever thought the picnic could be a pleasant little domestic interlude?

It had been a disaster! She'd stopped Callum from getting on with an important job and she'd embarrassed him in front of the men. And she'd forced him into the kind of intimate situation that they'd been trying so hard to avoid!

Heavens! She'd wanted Callum to kiss her again. For a moment she'd thought she might die if he didn't. Thank goodness he was stronger than she was.

With a guilty grimace she looked around her at the hideous scene she'd abandoned when she'd left the kitchen for the holding yards. The table top was still littered with the remains of her morning's efforts. Flour, spilled milk and sticky egg shells…strips of buttered paper she'd used for lining the cake tin…scales for weighing sugar and flour…a sieve, a bowl lined with hardening cake mix…and a trail of floury footprints criss-crossing the floor.

No doubt virtuous outback wives cleaned their kitchens instead of frolicking in the creek. Even Oscar in his cage in the corner seemed to be looking at her with an accusing eye.

'OK. OK,' she growled at him. 'I'm a messy cook.' Feeling belligerent, she plonked her hands on her hips. 'But the important thing that you mustn't forget, Oscar, is that *I am now a cook!* This is a red-letter day!'

Bending low, she peeked through the glass window in the oven door and admired her cake. Its surface was transforming exactly as it should from a gooey mess to a nicely golden-brown cake top. And it smelt superb!

So what if she'd made a mess of the kitchen? And so what if the picnic idea had been pathetic? At least her cake was baking beautifully!

Dramatically, she hurled her hands into the air and shouted at the top of her lungs, *'Stella Roper can cook! Oh, boy, can she cook! Hey, look at the way this woman can cook!'*

Pausing for breath, she realised to her horror that there was a knocking sound coming from somewhere beyond the kitchen.

'Hello,' a woman's voice called. 'Is that you, Stella?'

She froze. *Not a visitor. Not now.* Not when the place looked like the set of a disaster movie.

The knocking started up again.

Oh, help! Casting a despairing glance around the kitchen

she usually loved, she headed cautiously down the hall towards the front of the house.

Her stomach sank past her toes as she saw a middle-aged couple standing in the open front doorway and she recognised the well-televised, stern visage and impressive physique of the man. Tall and straight-backed, with the kind of thick, silver hair that always looked distinguished, Senator Ian Roper dominated the doorstep!

Oh, my God!

This sort of thing didn't happen. It just didn't. *Not to real people.* Parents-in-law couldn't just happen out of the blue, could they?

The woman beside him was smiling. She had youthfully brown and curly hair and her sleeveless black linen dress was simple but chic, a perfect foil for her long rope of chunky pearls.

Her smile was beaming as she stepped forward. 'You must be Stella,' she said, holding out her hand. 'I'm Margaret Roper, Callum's mother, and this is Ian.'

Stella stared stupidly at Callum's mother. 'How did you get here?' she asked. Oh, Lord. Where were her brains? 'I—I mean, hello. Hello, Mr and Mrs Roper. Senator Roper. What a—a pleasant surprise.' Cringe! First she'd been rude, now she was being overly sugary and polite.

Margaret Roper opened her arms. She kissed Stella's cheek and then, for a moment or two, she held her close. She smelt of something delicate and expensive, like a freshly delivered bouquet.

'I'm so sorry we didn't give you any warning,' she said, 'but we only accessed Callum's wonderful message this morning and, as Ian was already scheduled to fly to Mount Isa for a meeting, we couldn't resist coming out here to see you both the minute the meeting was over.'

Stella looked past them to the distant landing strip. A

small plane was parked there and her memory stirred. She'd heard a plane flying overhead when she'd been coming back from the stock yards, but she hadn't given it a moment's thought. In the city planes flew overhead all the time. And they landed at airports.

What she'd completely forgotten was that, in the outback, planes, like everything else, behaved differently. They landed at people's front doors.

'How—how lovely to see you. Please come in. I'm afraid Callum's busy working on fences down at the yards.'

'Is he working on his own?' the Senator asked with a narrow-eyed glance that made Stella quite sure she was undergoing some kind of secret test.

'Oh, no. There are men from Drayton Downs helping him.'

'Ian,' Margaret Roper chided gently. 'Don't bombard the poor girl with questions the minute you arrive.' Her warm honey-brown eyes twinkled as she turned back to Stella. 'I'm just so excited about you and Callum. I always knew that my dear boy would find someone special. And this has been such a whirlwind affair. I think that's so romantic!'

'Yes,' Stella murmured weakly. 'Callum just—swept me off my feet. Ah—come and sit in the lounge. I'll make a pot of tea.'

Despite the fact that her legs felt like limp spaghetti, she managed to lead the Ropers into the lounge. It felt incredibly awkward to be showing them through the house they had lived in for umpteen years before Callum's father went into politics.

The Senator settled himself into the armchair by the window with the air of a king claiming his throne. With a frown, he surveyed the room slowly and thoroughly. No doubt he was making sure she hadn't helped herself to any of the antique silver.

Margaret didn't sit down. 'Why don't you let me help?' she suggested.

'Please don't bother,' Stella urged and she winced to hear the desperate note in her voice. 'I—I'm in the middle of—of things—in the kitchen.'

'You've been baking,' Margaret said, sniffing the air and smiling.

'Smells good,' added the Senator.

'Yes,' Stella agreed. 'It's not quite ready yet.'

'Don't worry. We're not hungry,' Margaret assured her. 'But some tea would be divine. And Stella…' Margaret hesitated slightly '…we were hoping it wouldn't be too much of an imposition if we stayed tonight. There's a rodeo in Mount Isa and all the hotels are booked.'

Help! They couldn't stay. There was nowhere for them to sleep. She was in the guest room. Callum was in the main bedroom. There were only single beds in the other rooms! Stella felt as if her head might explode.

'Of course you can stay. That would be—lovely. I'll make that tea.' Stella fled.

She reached the kitchen at a flat run, her heart thumping wildly. *Don't panic! Think!*

Think priorities. What's more important? Hiding this disgraceful mess in the kitchen or hiding the fact that Callum and I aren't a blissfully happily-ever-after married couple?

A quick recollection of the dreamy, sentimental look on Margaret's face and she knew there was only one answer.

But that meant she had to ferret her gear out of the guest bedroom and into Callum's room. Her heart did a fair imitation of a ballerina's pirouette. It also meant that tonight she and Callum would have to share his room. *His bed.*

Best not to think about that now. That kind of thinking could fry a girl's brain.

Her hands shook as she filled the kettle, but she forced her thoughts into order. In her work, whenever she'd had to track and report a natural disaster like a cyclone, there'd been procedures to follow. Now she developed a quick mental list of procedures for this disaster.

One, make cups of tea. Two, empty her things out of the guest room and into a suitcase. Three, new sheets on the Ropers' bed. Four, clean kitchen. Between steps one and four, run to the lounge for snippets of meaningful conversation with the in-laws. Five—

Forget it. She would never make it to five.

Sundown. The last post was in place. Using a crowbar and a long-handled shovel, Callum tamped the earth hard around it while Ernie and Jim slipped the final rail home.

A good day's work.

'Are you coming up to the house for a beer?' Callum asked.

Ernie shook his head. 'Thanks, mate, but I think we better push off home.'

Callum considered trying to change their minds, but he knew the thought of Stella waiting up at the homestead was making the men coy. And, as he waved them off, he realised that the thought of Stella waiting at home was making him feel a few things, too.

Hot, hard and brainless would have to head the list. These days, just being around her was an ordeal. Looking at her and talking to her was sweet torture. He'd nearly gone mad at her blessed picnic. All he could think about had been hauling her close and pushing her down into that soft grass, taking her mouth, kissing her sense-less…making her want him.

Him. Not Scott.

Over and over, like a video recorder stuck on replay, he kept seeing the way it could happen: her hair, black and shiny against the velvet green grass; her eyes changing from cool grey to stormy smoke as he lowered himself over her; her lips, wide and sexy, parting to smile at him; her body, warm, becoming hot and tense with longing; her voice—her sultry, tough-girl voice urging him closer.

Damn! He didn't have enough brains to give himself a headache. He was such a fool!

Cursing, he tossed the crowbar and shovel into the back of the truck. *Damn you, Scott. Damn you for deserting your woman.*

What had Stella been playing at by coming down to the yard for a picnic?

As he stepped onto Birralee's back veranda, he heard voices and his first reaction was relief. Company. For once he was grateful. Visitors would be the distraction he needed. They would provide a buffer between himself and Stella.

But as his hand reached for the fly-screen door, ready to push it open, he froze. That was his mother's voice! *'Struth!* His parents were here with Stella! How on earth was she coping? How would *he* cope?

His parents had always looked on him as their steady, earnest son, the one who, even as a little tyke, had been eager to please them. If they discovered the truth behind this marriage, they would be devastated. His heart plummeted as he entered the kitchen.

But, if he'd had all day to think about this moment, he never would have come up with the scenario he found.

His mother, wearing an apron, was up to her elbows in washing-up water. Stella, looking pale and tired, was dry-

ing a huge mixing bowl, and on the table in front of her
was a range of sparkling clean cooking utensils. His father,
sitting at the far end of the table with newspapers spread
in front of him, was calmly peeling prawns.

Talk about surreal!

Everybody spoke at once. His mother began to explain
that, as her hands were wet, she couldn't hug him. Stella
was offering excuses he couldn't follow about tea and
changing sheets.

Eventually the hubbub died and his father looked at him
with a steely eye. 'You turned out to be a sly old dog,
son.'

Callum nodded and swallowed a constriction in his
throat. 'I take it you got my message about the—about
our—good news.'

'Darling, we're delighted,' Margaret said warmly and
he saw that her face was glowing.

Stuff this! It should have been such a happy moment,
but Callum felt a lead weight settle in his chest. It actually
hurt to see his mother looking so happy. She hadn't looked
like that since before Scott died and she was going to be
so disappointed when she eventually learned the truth
about him and Stella.

'You know you've done Margaret out of the biggest
wedding in the district,' his father said.

Callum tried to smile. 'Sorry, Mum. It was just one of
those things that happen out of the blue.'

'Love at first sight?' Margaret asked, her brown eyes
shining with excitement and pleasure.

More like lust at first sight. Callum squashed that
thought.

'It certainly took Stella and me by surprise,' he said. As
he spoke, he looked at Stella and forced a smile and the

answering wistful expression in her eyes made his heart spin.

He wanted to tell her he was sorry. Sorry he wasn't Scott. Sorry he hadn't prepared her for this. Sorry for the thousand probing questions his father was sure to ask.

But luckily, right now, the Senator had less threatening things on his mind. He gestured to the pile of prawns in front of him. 'Can't shake your hand, son. I've got seafood all over me. Bought these prawns in Mount Isa. Freshly caught and flown in from the gulf. Thought they might be good for tonight.'

'Excellent,' Callum managed. 'Saves cooking dinner.'

'We didn't want to arrive empty-handed,' Margaret added.

Callum's eyes returned to Stella. To his amazement, she put down the bowl she'd been drying and hurried towards him, flashing a tight smile. 'Darling, how was your day?' She raised her face to his for a kiss.

Blood pounded through his body.

Settle, boy. Don't overreact. This is simply a demonstration for the parents of how the little wife greets her husband at the end of the working day.

He kissed her cheek. 'Hi, sweetheart. I'm afraid I can't kiss you properly. I'm covered in dirt and dust.'

Fortunately, his parents laughed.

And with heightened colour in her cheeks and downcast eyes, Stella removed herself back to the far side of the kitchen.

He looked again at the collection of cooking gear. 'How did the cake turn out?'

'Don't ask!' three voices snapped in chorus. And any hint of pink drained from Stella's cheeks.

'No, Stella! Not the cake. What happened?'

She didn't answer at first, but her chin lifted in that

familiar, haughty way she adopted when things got tough and her eyes flashed him a warning. *Don't you dare make a joke about this!* 'It burned.'

'That's—that's really bad luck.' He cleared his throat. 'I'm sorry…but…if you'll excuse me, I'll go and have a shower. Make myself presentable.'

He hurried to his bedroom to collect clean clothes. Two steps into the room he saw Stella's suitcase poking out from under his bed and he came to a heart-thudding halt.

Her hairbrush and mirror were on his dresser. Stepping closer, he saw the little silver chain with its blue glass beads lying on the cut-glass tray that held his cuff-links.

His pulses leapt as he stepped into the adjoining bathroom and found her multicoloured toothbrush in the rack beside his.

He realised immediately what she had done and why, but his wave of admiration for her quick-thinking was rapidly swamped by a more pressing thought. If he and Stella had to follow through with this charade, he was facing the most difficult and potentially dangerous night of his life.

In bed with Stella.

CHAPTER SEVEN

CALLUM closed his bedroom door and leaned his back against it as he released a long sigh of relief. As far as he could tell, he and Stella had made it through the first part of the evening without any major mishaps.

But how to deal with the long night ahead? If he wasn't excruciatingly careful, this was where things could get really tricky.

Right now, Stella was standing in the middle of his bedroom with her arms crossed over her chest as if she half expected him to pounce on her.

'You were terrific tonight,' he told her. 'Anyone would think you'd had years of practice at being married.'

She gave a dismissive little laugh. 'I got an A for drama in high school.'

Easing himself away from the door, he tried not to think about his own performance this evening. Whenever she'd touched him, or when she'd called him 'darling', he'd tried to keep his breathing steady, but each touch, each look, each word, had made him want her more than ever.

'What happened when your father took you away for a man-to-man talk?' she asked.

'I thought he made a pretty good fist of coming to terms with his shock,' Callum admitted. 'His comments were all positive apart from chewing over the fact that we rushed into marriage without telling them.'

'Your mother told me they've been hoping you would settle down and—and start a family.'

'Yeah.' Callum sent her a wry grin. He'd heard that

message from his mother many times. 'Well, I'm halfway there.'

She was rubbing her left hand nervously up and down her right arm.

'I should have warned you that Mum would want to invite my sisters and their families to come over here tomorrow. But that's my family, I'm afraid. Any sniff of a chance for a celebration—'

Stella shrugged. 'She assures me that Ellie and Catherine are bringing enough food to feed an army, so at least I won't have to panic about a catering crisis.'

'That reminds me, I'm sorry about the cake.' She looked so suddenly miserable, he wanted to offer some comfort—a hug or even a pat on the shoulder—but any kind of touching was not a good idea tonight. He shoved his hands in his pockets. 'I know how much it meant to you.'

She blinked and gave a little shrug. 'I'm over it.'

'Nothing could be salvaged?'

'Your mother was very good. She helped me cut off the burnt top and sides. There's a bit in the middle that's not too bad.' Her lip curled in a twisted smile. 'It was going so well until they arrived.'

Exhaling a loud sigh, he looked around the room that had suddenly grown too small—way too small if it was to accommodate the two of them for a whole night. 'How on earth did you get all your gear out of the guest room and into here?'

'It was a dicey exercise.' She rolled her eyes. 'It's part of the reason I burned the cake. But what we've got to worry about now is—'

'How we spend the night,' Callum finished for her and he wondered what he could do about the way his body primed itself for action at the merest thought of having Stella share his bed.

'I'll get changed in the bathroom,' she offered.

'Sure. Good idea.'

With nervous haste, she pulled purple silk pyjamas from her suitcase and hurried through to the adjoining room.

Callum hunted through his drawer, searching for something that would serve as pyjamas. He usually slept bare, but tonight a strait-jacket or a suit of chain mail would come in handy. He settled for a pair of solid black cotton boxer shorts and changed into them quickly. Then he turned down the old fashioned, cotton waffle bedspread.

And Stella walked back into the room.

The purple silk of her pyjama top clung to her breasts and the short bottoms revealed far too much of the shapely length of her legs. Bright colour flared along her cheekbones. She looked as breathless and edgy as he felt.

He made a desperate decision. 'You take the bed. I'll be fine over there in the armchair.'

'You're sure?'

'Absolutely.' Snatching a spare pillow and a light throw from the top of the wardrobe, he hastily switched off the wall light and settled himself in the chair. 'This is great,' he lied.

Stella climbed onto his queen-size bed and sat to one side. In the light cast by the bedside lamp, she looked distinctly ill at ease. Sexy, desirable...but uneasy.

Across the room, they watched each other and the air seemed to throb with their tension.

'How are you going to sleep there?' she asked. 'Your legs are far too long.'

'Don't tempt me out of this chair, Stella.' He grimaced as he heard the unmistakable growl of desire in his voice.

She must have heard it, too, because she suddenly reached for the sheet and drew it over her legs.

Closing his eyes, Callum prayed for sanity. 'Why don't you tell me about Scott's visits to Sydney?' he suggested.

'I beg your pardon?'

'Scott never talked much about his trips away.' He needed to have his little brother where he belonged—as a fixed, immovable wedge—between them.

Perhaps she understood because, after a moment or two's hesitation, her shoulders seemed to relax against the pillows. 'What exactly do you want to know?'

'Whatever you're prepared to tell me. Of course, I only want a censored version.'

She raised both hands and ran them through her hair, lifting it and then letting it slip silkily back into place. It was a habit that seemed to help her relax and, no matter how many times she did it, Callum never tired of watching.

'Actually, I'm glad you've asked,' she said. 'I've been wanting to explain about that because I don't want you to get the wrong idea about me. Scott and I were—were just good friends for ages.' She pleated the sheeting with her fingers. 'I'd never met anyone like him. He was so much fun.'

Callum nodded. 'Scotty was fun all right.'

'One Saturday night, we went to a really exclusive Sydney Harbour restaurant and he pretended to be a prisoner just released from jail. He told the poor waiter I was his parole officer.'

'That'd be Scott.' Callum couldn't hold back his chuckle. 'He loved pulling pranks like that. I remember having dinner with him in a restaurant in Cairns once and he pretended to be a German tourist. He kept up the accent all evening.'

'I can imagine. He missed his calling as an actor. On our date he kept up this whole spiel about how much Sydney had changed in the five years he'd been "inside".'

He rattled on about how the items on the menu had become so cosmopolitan. I found myself playing along with him. We certainly fooled the restaurant staff.'

After a stretch of silence, she added softly. 'It's just terrible that he died.'

And wasn't that the truth.

She did the thing with her hair again and Callum's hands balled into fists. *Don't think about running your fingers there!*

He sighed. 'Scott liked to get away. I think he tended to think of living way out here as being in a kind of jail. Most of the time he didn't mind it, but every so often he just had to break out.'

Stella's expression was thoughtful as she lowered herself forward until she lay stomach-down on the mattress and propped her head on her hand. Over the end of the bed, she looked at him with searching directness. 'I would have thought living in the city was more like being in jail. Out here there's so much freedom. Nobody breathing down your neck. How do you feel about living here?'

'There's no other place I'd rather be.'

'That's what I guessed,' she said softly. 'I think I'd feel that way too. If I really belonged here.' She traced the geometric pattern of the folded bedspread with one finger. 'But I've never really belonged anywhere.'

Their gazes reconnected and held. What was she saying? Callum didn't dare think. She couldn't possibly mean she wanted to go on living here with him. His heart almost stopped at the thought of having her here in his life, his wife for ever, the mother of his children...

But no, that definitely wasn't what she was saying.

'Where do your family live?' he asked.

She groaned and dropped her head so that her hair fell and covered her face. 'Please, let's not talk about that.'

After a puzzled pause, he shrugged. 'If you insist.'
Every time the subject of her family came up she behaved
the same way. He knew her anxiety about cooking was
somehow tied up with this family of hers. He suspected
that her agreeing to leave her baby behind was connected
to that, too.

'One of these days I'll tell you about my mother,' she
said.

'OK,' he said softly, hoping she couldn't tell how exceptionally pleased he was by this very small sign of trust.

'But tonight's not the time.'

'Perhaps we should try to sleep.'

'I suppose so.'

She sounded doubtful and he was secretly relieved.
Truth was, he could go on listening to her husky, honeyed
voice all night. It wound around him like wood smoke
from a warming camp fire.

'Unless you want to tell me some more about Scott,' he
said, wondering just when he'd become partial to self-
inflicted pain.

She seemed to consider this suggestion, then shrugged
her shoulders. 'Well—there was one wet Sunday I'll never
forget. My flatmate went to watch her boyfriend play foot-
ball in the rain and Scott and I stayed in my apartment and
had pizzas delivered and listened to music and—'

Made love. His stomach crawled. 'It's OK. You don't
have to tell me every intimate detail.'

Stella ignored him. 'And I painted Scott's toenails.'

Her words hit him like a grenade going off in his face.
'You what?'

She smiled shyly. 'I know it sounds wacky. A big tough
bush bloke letting me paint his toenails just for fun.'

Hell! He struggled to breathe. Never had he been so

painfully aware of the vast difference between himself and his young brother.

Callum knew there was absolutely no way he could get involved in toenail painting with a woman. And it wasn't that he was hung up about gender roles. It was the sheer intimacy of the act.

Sure, sex was intimate…but sex was intense and fuelled by passion. It wasn't the same as being so totally at ease with a woman as to be able to do something as off-the-wall and unexpectedly personal as having one's toenails painted! Just for fun!

I'm so tied up in knots I couldn't even enjoy her simple picnic.

In his mind's eye, he could see Scott and Stella together. He could hear the private laughter, the jokes; he could sense the touching, the shared companionship. Suddenly he felt desperately lonely and hopelessly inadequate as a stand-in for his brother.

'What colour?' he managed to ask at last.

'Colour?'

'The nail polish.'

'I'm not sure if I remember. It was a shade of red. I think it was ruby.'

His voice shook slightly as he asked, 'Is that why you want to call your baby Ruby?'

Stella looked surprised, as if the link had never occurred to her. 'I don't think so. I just think Ruby's a cute name.'

They lapsed into an awkward silence.

'Callum, there's something else I should explain about Scott.'

He braced himself mentally for bad news. 'Explain away.'

'It's just that Scott and I split up—before I knew I was pregnant.'

He stared at her, unable to speak.

'It was pretty awful. You see I finally realised that I'd been clinging to a relationship that just wasn't going to work. I'd been hoping that Scott would settle down... He was fun, but he didn't want to get serious...'

What a joke! How ironical could life get? Callum's fists clenched. Here he was, bursting to get serious with Stella and she was still breaking her heart over Scott, who'd been terminally allergic to getting serious with a woman. 'I'm sorry if my little brother hurt you, Stella.'

She didn't answer.

The chiming clock in the lounge struck midnight and from beyond the homestead came the soft call of a mopoke.

'I guess we'd better get some sleep,' she said.

'Yeah.' He tried to settle his long body into the cramped chair. 'Goodnight.'

''Night, Callum.'

After a minute or two, she switched off the lamp and he could hear her movements as she made herself comfortable in the bed.

Then silence. No sound but the wind in the trees. No light except for faint bars of creamy moonshine seeping through the slats in the blinds. He closed his eyes and tried to ignore the pain in his heart and the disturbing pressure in his loins. Just as well he was cramped up in this chair. A little discomfort might straighten out his useless, X rated thoughts.

There was more silence till the lounge clock chimed a quarter past the hour.

Then, through the darkness, came Stella's voice, low and excited. 'Callum, come here.'

He jolted upright, peering through the pale light cast by the moon. She'd kicked the sheet away and was lying on her side, holding her hand against her lower abdomen. He stared, but didn't move.

'Are you all right?'

'Yes, but come here. Quickly.'

'Stella, I—'

'It might stop soon.'

'What is it?'

'The baby. At least I think it's the baby. There's this tiny little flutter-kick thing happening down here.'

'Are you sure you want me to—?'

'Yes, hurry.'

Crossing the floor quickly, he sat on the side of the bed. Stella grabbed his hand and, slipping it under the waist-band of her pyjama bottoms, pressed it firmly against her lower stomach.

Sweat broke out all over him! So close to the most womanly part of her! He was trembling as his palm pressed against her soft…smooth…warm…luscious…skin. Heaven help him! She felt so sensual…so good.

'You have to push me in a bit because it's still quite little, but can you feel that?'

Drawing on will-power he didn't know he had, he ignored how incredibly sexy this moment was and concentrated on the tiny movement bumping against his palm. He held his breath and the movement came again. And again. Like the soft bump of a duckling's bill tapping the inside of an egg. 'Yes,' he whispered huskily. 'I can. I can feel it.'

She looked up at him and her face was so close he could feel her soft breath against his cheek and he could see the warm, vulnerable sense of wonder in her eyes.

'It's Ruby,' she whispered.

He wanted to kiss her. Oh, God! He wanted to kiss her from head to toe. 'It's going to be a perfect little baby,' he whispered back and still he wanted to kiss her. Yes, he would start by kissing her pretty toes and then he'd move slowly up her long silky legs. Or perhaps he would start at her mouth and then move down. Either way, he would explore every sweet and secret part of her. This was Stella and she was so lovely, so gutsy, so maddeningly sexy. So near!

And she was looking at him with eyes swimming with emotion. Her soft lips were parted in sensual invitation. *They were married.* Married and alone in bed together. There was absolutely no reason on earth that they couldn't kiss.

He'd never desired any other woman the way he wanted Stella. He edged closer.

Come to your senses, man! Hell! Wake up! Think about Scott! She chose Scott, not you! Besides, you made her a promise that this wouldn't happen!

Seconds from making the worst mistake possible, he withdrew his hand from her warmth and softness and slid from the bed to stand beside her, hands safely on his hips.

'That was an enlightening experience,' he said and winced as he heard how sarcastic and rude that sounded.

She looked understandably hurt. 'I wanted to share a special moment with you.'

'I know,' he said more gently. 'I—er—' How could he explain to her what he couldn't explain to himself? His thoughts were plunging and scattering like tumbleweed in a storm.

He was trying so hard not to say something really stupid. He wanted, he needed, to make love to her. Right now! But he also wanted to love and protect her in the future as much as he wanted to love and protect her baby, but if he said that, she'd pack up and run. She didn't want his love. All she wanted from him was a roof over her baby's head.

She pulled the sheet back over her. 'Look,' she said huffily when she was safely covered up, 'I told you all that stuff about Scott because I thought that getting everything out in the open would be good for both of us.'

He nodded.

'So we can put this pretend marriage into its proper perspective.'

'Which perspective would that be?'

'Well—Scott and I weren't careful enough. We made a silly, immature mistake but, thanks to this arrangement, you and I can go part way to correcting it. This marriage is a practical and adult solution,' she said solemnly.

'Oh, yeah. I'm—glad you see it that way.'

'But if we're going to keep on being practical and adult, you can't spend the night in that chair. It's ridiculous.'

Callum coughed. 'Stella, give me a break. If I got into bed with you it would be very—very adult, but I'm not sure it's practical.'

Passionate, deep thrusting sex could hardly be described as practical. Unless there was a baby to be made…

And that had already been accomplished by his brother.

Stella lay stiffly with her arms folded across her chest as if for protection. 'There's plenty of room here. You take that side of the bed, I'll stick to my half, and we should both get some sleep.'

Sleep? Sure…as if I won't notice the minuscule space separating your luscious, semi-naked body from mine.

'We both know nothing's going to happen,' she said tightly.

'Of course!' he replied, too quickly and way too loudly!

CHAPTER EIGHT

STELLA lay beside Callum, stiff as a mummified corpse, staring at the ceiling. Wide awake. There was no way she could relax and drop off to sleep.

She was too aware of Callum in her bed. Oh, man! The picnic had been difficult enough, but now! He looked ultra-divine wearing nothing but skimpy boxer shorts. And he was just here, in easy reach!

For the sake of her sanity, she had to drag her mind away from those dangerous thoughts. She pressed her hand against the warm little mound of her growing baby and couldn't help smiling into the dark as it responded with yet another little thump. Tiny Ruby. Somehow she was sure it was a girl. What a cute little mover her baby was.

But still, she hadn't been prepared for the way those little movements made her feel. Most of the time she only allowed herself to think of her pregnancy as a kind of inconvenient illness, but tonight it really hit her that this was a proper little person she carried inside her.

And suddenly she could visualise it clearly. At first it would be tiny and cute and helpless like a baby doll, but in a few short years her baby would be a laughing, impish child. A skinny and long-limbed outback tomboy with sun-streaked curls and a freckled nose.

Her throat tightened painfully as she thought about Ruby growing up with Callum and the rest of the Ropers.

Without her.

Ruby would have Callum to watch over her and love her and teach her to ride. Stella could picture them charging off on horseback together across Birralee's vast plains. Tough and free and open-hearted like the country they loved.

And where would she be?

Alone in a city somewhere?

Alone as she'd been for most of her life?

Her mother had thrown away her only doll in one of her drunken rages. And now she was going to give this baby away.

She bunched the sheet into a ball and shoved it into her mouth to stop herself from moaning aloud. How aching and empty she felt.

How could she bear the thought of other arms holding her little one? Other ears hearing her laughter, her first word...seeing her first steps...comforting her...knowing the warmth of her chubby arms.

But it was *her* baby! How could she have ever thought it was right to give it away? How could she let Callum's family become the most important people in her child's world?

If only...

She turned her head to look at the dark silhouette of Callum's shoulder as he lay on his side with his back to her. Each day that passed, she felt more and more drawn to him in every way. If only he had married her for a more romantic reason than his sense of duty to Scott!

If only they could be like a normal married couple—lovers who raised their baby in their own little close-knit family. But that wasn't what he'd planned at all. Callum married her for one reason—to give the baby legitimacy and to raise it at Birralee. Sure, he was attracted to her physically. But he'd made it clear that his prime interest was Scott's baby. Not her.

With a groaning sigh she rolled over in the other direction and stared at the far wall. Tomorrow his sisters and their husbands and children would arrive. So much family. So many questions.

Help!

By noon the next day, Birralee's huge kitchen looked and sounded like something out of one of Stella's fantasies.

Every chair around the table was occupied and the table was laden with food. Excited talk and laughter filled the room and drifted out through the windows that were opened wide to catch the breeze.

As she'd expected, Callum's sisters were attractive and capable. Their husbands were predictably tall, sun-tanned and good-looking, and their children healthy and glowing. To her relief, everyone was amazingly friendly. They hugged Stella and welcomed her into their fold without a moment's hesitation.

It was actually frightening to see how easily they accepted her and how naturally they assumed she was wonderful—as if Callum would only choose the most suitable, very best woman to be his wife.

His younger sister Ellie kissed Stella and stood holding her by the arms and looking deeply into her eyes. Her own eyes were the same warm toffee as Callum's and they glowed as she said, 'Oh, yes, Stella, you're so perfect for Callum. I can feel it in my bones.'

Stella thanked heavens for her years of practice at hiding her innermost thoughts and feelings. Those times helped her now as she returned Ellie's frank gaze. She hoped her smile was friendly and assured, even though her mind was whispering, *I'm a fake. I'm a fake. I'm a big fat fake.*

How bitterly disappointed this family would be when she left Callum! Stella clung to the faint hope that, eventually, the baby she left behind would make up for her sins.

Her self-esteem wasn't helped by the discovery that Ellie and Catherine were as gifted in the kitchen as she suspected and they'd brought a mountain of gourmet delights—home-made sausages wrapped in bread for the children and cold roast beef with a special pepper crust for the adults.

And the accompaniments were just as impressive—white radish and wild rocket salad and spicy coriander rice. There was even dessert—crunchy biscotti and a soft meringue roll oozing raspberry-flavoured mascarpone.

Stella had never seen a meal quite like it outside a restaurant and, all the time she ate, she kept recalling her blackened cake and Margaret Roper's initial shock when she'd discovered the state of the kitchen yesterday.

Thankfully, that was behind her. Today Oscar's cage had been moved to a hook just outside the back door and she'd scoured the kitchen until once again it was the epitome of country charm.

Ellie's daughter, Penny, occupied the high chair and she beamed at everyone like a baby princess on her throne, looking impossibly cute as she solemnly speared pieces of cold sausage and halved cherry tomatoes with her fork.

Every so often Ellie would lean over and help her baby. She would kiss Penny's round cheek and the little girl would dimple with delight. At one point they rubbed noses and laughed into each other's faces and the perfect, open love that passed between the two of them made Stella's eyes sting.

That could be me. Ruby and I could be like that. She struggled to block out memories of Marlene sobbing, 'I want to be a good mother but I don't know how.'

Maybe I don't know how either, Mother. You never showed me the way.

Oh, Lord! This kind of thinking would send her into a mess! Closing her eyes, she took a deep breath and willed her nerves to settle. If only she'd had a chance to talk to Callum about a plan of attack for handling this meal.

He was sitting beside her and, at that moment, he squeezed her hand and the skin on her arms prickled warmly. Leaning close, he whispered, 'How are you holding out?'

She turned slightly to meet his gaze and he traced a pattern on her palm with his thumb. His touch and the understanding in his eyes made her as warm and melting as a birthday candle. Goodness, he was good at this! No wonder his family believed he really loved her.

Margaret was sitting opposite them, watching them fondly. She reached across the table and patted Callum's free hand. Her eyes shone and her mouth wobbled a little, but she smiled bravely as she said, 'Callum, darling, how clever of you to discover Stella. You've found such a wonderful way to help us get over—over Scotty.'

Stella's face flamed and a weird choking cry forced its way from her throat.

Callum quickly drew her head against his shoulder, dropping warm kisses on her forehead as he did so and she was grateful that her hair fell forward, creating a shielding curtain that hid her face.

'Stella knew Scotty, too,' she heard him explain to his mother, and, feeling dreadful, she kept her flushed face pressed into the warm hollow of his shoulder. 'That's how—how we met.'

'What did you say Stella's maiden name was, Callum?' came the Senator's voice, booming from the far end of the table.

Her head shot up and her dismay was replaced by a new fear. Was this the moment when everything came completely unstuck? How many questions would she have to answer about her family?

'My name was Lassiter,' she told her father-in-law and she realised that every adult at the table was listening and watching her carefully.

'Lassiter,' he repeated with a thoughtful frown. 'So does that mean you're related to the Lassiters who own Janderoo station over near Pentland? Don and Freda Lassiter? They come from a big family.'

'No,' Stella answered hastily. 'I don't think so. My people have always been city folk.'

'Callum's not one for the city, so how did you two meet?' This came from Catherine. Her eyes were very dark and piercing like her father's and Stella suddenly felt like a squirming bug impaled by an entomologist's scalpel. All she could think of was the truth—that she had met Callum once at a party and then had told him she'd preferred his brother.

To her relief, Callum answered his sister for her. 'Scott introduced us. Then Stella came up here on holiday and I kind of moved in on her.' He turned to her again and sent her a beautiful, tummy-flipping smile.

'Smartest move you ever made, brother,' cheered Ellie.

'Yeah.' He flung an arm around Stella's shoulders.

'Sweetheart!' There was a broken note in Margaret's voice. 'It's so lovely to know that Scott played a part in your happiness with Stella. Somehow it feels so right.'

Help! Stella focused downcast eyes on the lacy pattern of the tablecloth in front of her. Deceiving this fine, grieving woman was terrible. Putting Callum in a position where he had to deceive his own mother was unforgivable!

A momentary respite was provided by the children, who

had eaten their fill and were becoming bored. As they gained permission to leave the table and to run on the veranda or explore the garden outside, the adults settled down to coffee. A platter of cheese and fruit was handed around.

But before Stella could relax, Catherine's husband, Rob, fired another question her way.

'What kind of work did you do in the city, Stella?'

For a moment her mind froze, scared that the truth might be her undoing, that somehow everything about the London job would come out. But to her intense relief, when she mentioned her background in meteorology, the conversation actually steered into safer waters. Soon everyone was discussing the outback cattleman's favourite topic—the weather.

Stella understood the fragile, dependent relationship people on the land shared with the elements and she soon became totally absorbed in discussions about tropical cyclones, bush fires, severe thunderstorms, floods and droughts.

In fact, she found herself the centre of attention as she outlined some of the ways meteorological research could support the cattle industry to plan the best uses for their land and water resources.

There were murmurs of agreement. Senator Roper was watching her with a narrowed-eyed, speculative gaze, but she tried not to let it unnerve her.

Ellie grinned broadly. 'This gal of yours is much more than a pretty face, Callum.'

She saw a flash of agreement in the eyes of the others at the table, but she held her hands out to indicate the remains of the spread in front of them. 'But I can't cook.'

And there was a ripple of indulgent laughter.

Eventually, the meal drew to a close and Stella could feel the knots in her stomach beginning to loosen a little.

'Now, let's attack the dishes,' Ellie suggested.

'Please don't,' Stella cried. 'I didn't prepare one crumb of the food, so I want you to leave the clearing and the washing-up to me.'

'We can't leave you with all this,' interjected a horrified Catherine. 'We always pitch in.'

'That's how families do things in the bush,' added Ellie with a grin.

Families? For a moment, Stella almost faltered. Perhaps she was breaking some ancient family law? But then she shook her head and insisted, 'Honestly, thanks for the offer, but I'd like to look after this.' After all, a girl had to have some pride. She felt bad enough eating all their food.

There were more protests but, eventually, they gave in. While Stella remained alone in the kitchen, they wandered outside to round up their children, search for discarded shoes or socks and to talk about hitting the road if they wanted to be home before dark.

Stella was busily stacking plates on the draining board when she heard heavy footsteps behind her. She turned and her heart tripped several beats when she saw Senator Roper standing quite close.

'I wondered if I could have a quick word, Stella?'

Oh, crumbs! 'Of course.'

Without smiling, he gestured towards any empty chair at the half-cleared table. 'Please, take a seat.'

She gulped. 'Thank you.' Then she sat with her damp palms clasped in her lap.

At first she was afraid he was going to remain standing but, to her relief, he drew out a chair and sat facing her. His face remained as serious as a heart attack. 'My son seems to have lost his head over you,' he said.

She was so surprised and alarmed, she couldn't think of one sensible word to offer in response.

'My wife is a romantic,' Senator Roper continued. 'She's over the moon about this marriage. But I know my son. I know it's totally out of character for Callum to behave this way—on a whim. And I have to admit that I was extremely surprised that he rushed so quickly into marriage with a woman who was prepared to tell him so little of her background.'

Stella's chin lifted. She guessed that her background would have been of vital importance to this man. Well, that was too bad! She wasn't about to enlighten him.

Her cheeks were hot, but she hoped she didn't look anywhere near as frightened as she felt. 'Your son didn't require details of my pedigree before he asked me to be his wife.'

Her father-in-law's eyes widened.

'Are you telling me you're unhappy with his choice?' she challenged.

He shook his head, but there was no softening in his expression. 'If my son really loves you, that is enough.'

But it obviously wasn't enough. The Senator's eyes narrowed as he went on. 'But I must warn you, Stella, that Callum is a man whose feelings run deep. He still mourns the loss of his brother profoundly.'

'Yes, I do realise that.'

'His emotions are probably more vulnerable now than they have been at any other time.'

'I understand.'

He watched her carefully through an uncomfortable minute of silence. What could she say? If he had been hoping to make her feel small and guilty, he'd succeeded.

He rose and offered her his hand. 'All I'm asking is that you take care of him for us, Stella.'

There was still no smile and she fancied she could hear what he *wasn't* saying: *If you hurt the only son I have left, I'll never forgive you.*

She wasn't sure if her legs would support her as she tried to stand. She could only force one reluctant smile. 'I promise you, I want the best for Callum, too,' she told him.

They shook hands and with a curt little nod of his head he turned and left the room as quickly as he'd entered.

Stella sagged against the sink, feeling ill. She knew that Callum had made an enormous sacrifice of his own pride and dignity by marrying her, but the worst was yet to come—after the baby was born, when she left him to face his family.

Oh, Lord! She should never have agreed to this marriage. Callum had been so insistent that it was the best decision, and at the time it had seemed like the right solution for the baby, but now she just felt terribly selfish— as if she was merely using Callum to suit her own ends!

Turning to the dishes in the sink, she attempted to finish the task of stacking plates, but her hands were shaking so much she feared she might break them.

Then there were more footsteps heading her way and she turned to see Ellie hurrying into the room.

'We'll be heading off soon,' she said.

Stella nodded. 'Thank you so much for coming.' She spoke quickly, feeling totally out of her depth as she struggled to shrug aside the aftershocks of her conversation with the Senator and to adopt the calm warmth required of a hostess. 'The food was superb. I don't know how you did it at such short notice.'

'Oh, all sorts of things can be managed at short notice,' Ellie replied with a knowing sparkle in her eyes. 'Even weddings.'

'Well, yes. I guess so.'

Ellie's hand rested on Stella's arm. 'I know your secret,' she said softly.

'You do?' Stella's nervous stomach bunched into even tighter knots. What secret could Ellie know? That the marriage was a sham? That Stella was going to walk out on Callum in a few months' time? That she would be leaving him holding a baby that wasn't even his?

Oh, Lord! Ellie couldn't know about Scott, could she? Could he have told his sister about his visits to Sydney? Her heart fluttered in her chest like Oscar flapping in his cage.

'You're pregnant, aren't you?' Ellie said.

Stella's hand flew to her stomach. 'How—how did you know?'

The other woman's mouth twisted in a wry smile. 'I've been there three times. I know the signs. You didn't touch the alcohol or the coffee. You avoided any of the smoked and soft cheeses—just ate the crackers on their own. You've got a glow.'

'A *glow*?'

Ellie laughed. 'It's nothing toxic. Not a glow-in-the-dark kind of glow—just a nice bloom in your cheeks. I always think we women look our best when we're pregnant.'

Stella didn't know what to say. She really liked Ellie. From the moment they'd met she'd felt a genuine kinship, but she doubted the friendliness would last if Callum's sister knew the whole truth.

'When are you due?' Ellie asked.

Stella hesitated. Admitting to dates could incriminate her—but then so would avoiding the question. Her baby was due in October, but she added a couple of weeks to her dates and left her answer vague. 'Before Christmas.'

Ellie frowned. 'Callum might need to do a final muster

before the wet season sets in. Could be dicey. Have you booked into Mount Isa hospital or are you going in to the coast?'

'We haven't really talked about that yet.'

They could hear Ellie's husband, Andrew, calling to her. 'Coming,' she called back. To Stella she said, 'Better get all the hospital stuff sorted out straight away. It can catch up with you sooner than you think.'

'OK. I will. Thanks.' Stella followed her out of the kitchen. In the doorway, she said, 'Ellie, I haven't wanted to broadcast news about the baby just yet.'

'I don't blame you. Dad's a bit of a dinosaur. Let him get used to one bit of startling news at a time.' She slipped an arm around Stella's shoulder and gave it a squeeze. 'I'm just so wrapped about you and Callum. Anyone can see how into each other you two are.'

Gulp! Stella managed an awkward smile and nodded and then they joined everyone on the front veranda and soon she was absorbed in the general fuss and clamour of farewells. The two young families piled into their four-wheel drive vehicles and Callum's parents headed off for the light plane which Senator Roper would fly back to Mount Isa.

Stella and Callum were left standing alone at the top of Birralee's steps. She felt exhausted, confused and guilty.

'Thank God that's over,' Callum said, staring grimly at the diminishing speck of his parents' aircraft.

They were alone again. All around them stretched the wide, silent plains and the even wider, more silent skies of the outback. Alone—surrounded by an ancient land—trees, rocks and sky—and not another human within eighty kilometres.

Maybe Callum was thinking about this, too. In profile, his face was hard and stony and, when he looked at her, the warmth that had filled his eyes at lunch-time was replaced by a cold, bleak regret. She guessed at once that he was feeling very badly about so much deception.

'Thank you for covering for me,' she said.

His sigh was long, loud and bitter. 'I know this marriage was my idea, but I didn't enjoy pulling the wool over my parents' eyes.'

Before she could respond, he strode away as if he couldn't bear to talk about it. With leaden steps, and an even heavier heart, she went back into the house to do her penance at the mountain of dirty dishes in the kitchen.

A fortnight later, a letter arrived from Callum's father. Stella left it on the sideboard with the other mail, and when Callum came home in the evening she watched as he stood, with his back to her, slit the envelope and scanned the hand-written page. She saw his deep frown and a tremor of fear skittered through her.

When he'd finished, he folded the letter slowly and then examined other pages of printed matter that had come with it. Finally, he thrust everything back in the envelope and stood tapping it against his thigh as he stared at the floor.

She had to ask. 'Is something the matter?'

He sighed. 'You may as well read it.' Unsmiling, he handed her the envelope.

'Are you sure you want me to?'

He nodded, but he looked so unhappy her hands shook as she pulled the fine sheet of letter paper away from the others and read.

Dear Callum,
Because of the speed with which you married (which in my view fell just short of elopement), your mother and I haven't had a chance to give you a wedding

present.

*As you know, Birralee has been in the family for al-
most one hundred years and it would have been going
to you and Scott eventually. I made handsome settle-
ments on the girls when they were married. And so, son,
Callum Angus Roper is now the official owner of the
family's business. Birralee Pastoral Company is yours.
It's all signed and sealed.*

*Look after the place and it will take care of you. And
just make sure that you and Stella get on with the job
of raising a family so you can hand it on when the time
comes.*

Love,
Dad

Stella read the letter through twice. She felt terrible.
Callum's family were placing so much weight on this marriage. 'You weren't expecting anything like this?' she
asked.

He shrugged. 'I doubt it would have happened if Scott
hadn't died. Knowing my old man, it probably wouldn't
have happened if I hadn't married.'

'You don't sound very happy.'

'I don't know. I can see Mum's hand in all this and I—'
He clamped his lips together as if he had to hold back
what he really wanted to say.

'You wish you could have told her the truth.'

He gave another shrug.

She hated to see him looking so unhappy. Especially
when it was her fault. 'Why don't you let me tell your
parents what we're doing?'

He couldn't have looked more shocked if she'd announced that she wanted to discuss their situation on talk-
back radio.

'Not now,' he snapped. 'They couldn't handle it. It'll be different when there's a grandchild. That will help to make up for—' His fists clenched, and for a long tortuous moment he stared at her.

'—For their disappointment when they realise you didn't marry for love?' Stella supplied.

His eyes seemed to burn into her and she sensed that he was struggling with a vicious inner demon. Then his lip curled. 'My mother's always been a hopeless romantic. She loves weddings. But she loves babies, too. She'll be tickled pink about your baby.'

Her baby. *The Roper family's baby.* A cold shiver crept through her and settled around her heart as she pictured her baby surrounded by Scott's family.

Now that she'd met them, she could fill in details. She could see their faces, voices and mannerisms. Her baby would love them and she'd be a sunshiny, happy soul just like Ellie's Penny.

Except…except…among those people who hugged and loved her baby…its mother would be missing.

Oh, hell! Her whole body was trembling. She had to shake that thought aside. It wouldn't do to give in to self-pity at this stage of the project, when it was Callum who deserved her concern.

For her, the future held adventure and hope—the TV documentary and who knew what else? But Callum had little choice about his future. Between them, she, Scott and his parents had put restrictions on his life, until they'd reduced it to something as predictable and unvarying as the ebb and flow of the tides. Callum would work Birralee and raise her child.

She watched him now as he stood stiffly in the middle of the room. 'I've never asked what you had planned for your future before—before I came along and made a mess of your life.'

He looked away. 'No use talking about what might have been.'

'When I'm gone, maybe you'll—get married again. I mean, properly married.' Nervously, she ran her hands through her hair.

'Maybe.' For another scorching minute, his burning gaze returned to her. He stared at her hands as she fiddled with her hair and she found herself dropping them behind her back.

'Your family will forgive you, Callum,' she said gently, searching for ways to soothe his obvious pain. 'They *love* you.'

A muscle pulsed in his cheek, but he didn't answer.

Stella rushed on, trying to find words to make him feel better, to make them both feel better. 'When they realise why you married me—that you did it out of love for Scott and his baby—they won't be angry with you.'

Again, he said nothing. In tormented silence, she watched as he put the letter in his pocket and walked out of the room.

CHAPTER NINE

FOR Callum, the day-to-day business of living with Stella got harder and harder. On the surface things were fine. She became much more confident with cooking and meal times became something to look forward to.

She also became totally involved in researching the management methods of some of the really big cattle companies, and they talked for hours about his growing vision for Birralee now that it was in his sole care.

At times he got the feeling that she really loved the challenge of the outback, but then he worried that she was trying so hard at cooking and learning about station life to help her forget about Scott and to ward off her unhappiness.

And, each day, it became more and more difficult to hide his feelings for her. His efforts to avoid touching her bordered on the ridiculous. It was more than a straight physical thing. His mother had recognised that. She knew he was deeply in love with Stella and she'd told him how happy she was that he'd found the right woman at last.

But when Stella left him, his family would know that his heart was broken and the burden of this impending disappointment made his own situation worse.

What a mess! What a crazy, hopeless mess!

Time was marching on. Stella's figure was changing. In Callum's eyes, she grew more womanly, more beautiful each day as her shape expanded, but luckily she seemed unaware of his fascination.

Books on pregnancy and new clothes arrived for her and

she modelled up and down the veranda. Dropping her gaze to her round tummy, she gave it a little pat. 'At least I'm starting to look pregnant and not just as if I've eaten too much.'

He wanted to tell her she looked gorgeous. Softer, sweeter—more womanly and desirable than ever. But what could be more stupid than messing up their careful plans with talk that sounded like seduction?

At times it was a relief to get away. He threw himself into new strategies for the management of Birralee, and one of his first decisions to help streamline production was to contract a top cattle vet to spey the female cattle he had ready for the live export market.

He hired Joe Ford whose new speying technique was basically painless and much faster than any method Callum was familiar with. The task was accomplished in a day. As they drove back to the homestead in the evening, Stella came flying down the back steps.

'Oh, thank heavens you're still here,' she said to Joe as he clambered out of the truck.

'What's the problem?' Callum's heart picked up pace when he saw her wild-eyed, worried look.

'It's Oscar.'

He frowned. 'Oscar?'

'Yes. He's looking terribly sick.'

Embarrassed, Callum explained to the vet. 'Oscar's a pet budgerigar.'

Joe cleared his throat. 'I—I see.'

Wringing her hands together, Stella pleaded, 'Can you come and take a look at him, please? I'm afraid he's dreadfully sick.'

'Stella, Joe's a cattle vet. He's not a budgerigar doctor. I don't think—'

Whirling back to face Callum, her eyes flashed sparks.

'A vet's a vet and Oscar needs a vet. Surely vets are like doctors.' She shot a sharp glance in Joe's direction. 'Don't you take some kind of oath to protect all animal life?'

Joe gave a helpless shrug. 'I'll take a quick look.'

'Thank you.' Hurrying ahead, she led the way to the kitchen and very soon all three of them were staring at the bird as it huddled on the bottom of the cage looking thoroughly miserable.

'He certainly looks pretty crook,' Callum admitted.

'You can do something, can't you?' Stella asked Joe. Her grey eyes were pleading and her face was far too pale.

Joe looked quite shamefaced as he shook his head. 'I'm sorry, but I don't think I can.'

She stared at him, appalled. 'But you have to. You're a vet. If you can fix a great big bull, surely you can fix a tiny little bird!'

'That's the trouble,' Joe said, shuffling his feet uncomfortably. 'I specialise in large animals. Large-animal vets are quite separate from small—'

Stella didn't wait to hear more. 'In Sydney when Oscar was sick, I took him to an excellent female vet and she weighed him in a little basket so she could tell how bad he was. Surely we can find some way to weigh him? I remember she told me that a healthy bird weighs about forty grams, but a sick one might only be thirty.'

Callum did his manful best to keep a straight face and wondered what Joe was making of this.

'She gave him antibiotics in a little plastic syringe and he was completely better in three days.'

'I'm sorry, but I don't carry antibiotics for budgerigars. Anything I have would kill him.'

She groaned melodramatically. 'I can't believe this! Honestly, who in their right minds would choose to live in the outback? Are you telling me there's absolutely nothing you can do for him?'

'If you keep him quiet and clean, he might recover.'

She ran a distracted hand through her hair and blinked her eyes.

'Stella,' Callum said. 'The trees out here are full of budgerigars. There are thousands of them—'

'*What are you saying?*' she yelled. 'I hope you're not suggesting that there's plenty more where Oscar came from.'

'I guess—I—'

'You have absolutely no idea what he means to me.'

She dashed out of the room leaving the two men to exchange embarrassed grimaces.

After Joe had flown off, Callum went to look for her and found her in the study, examining the spines of the books lined along the shelves. A pile of discarded books lay on the floor beside her.

'Don't you have anything about animal health?' she muttered between tensely gritted teeth.

'I really don't think we have anything that covers budgerigars.'

She let out an exasperated sigh and stood with her eyes downcast, her arms folded over the mound of her tummy and her chin jutting at a belligerent angle. Her foot tapped impatiently.

'I'm sorry, Stella. I shouldn't have said that about the other birds. I know how much Oscar means to you. You went to all the trouble of bringing him up here from Sydney and I've seen how carefully you look after him.'

'How would you feel if it was Mac?' she demanded.

'I'd be pretty cut up,' he admitted and tactfully refrained from adding any clichés about a man's best friend.

He searched for ways to distract her from worrying

about the bird but, no matter how hard he tried, he couldn't find the right words to cheer her. She stayed upset for the rest of the evening. Dinner was a very tense and tight-lipped affair.

Next morning, when Callum came into the kitchen, he saw immediately that Oscar hadn't improved. The bird was still huddled on the floor of the cage.

He heard Stella's footsteps coming down the hall. 'How is he?' she asked, white-lipped.

'Not much better, I'm afraid.'

'Oh, Callum, what are we going to do?' She stood beside the cage staring at the poor little creature, her restless fingers trailing helplessly up and down the bars of his cage.

Callum squeezed her shoulders gently. 'There's still a chance that he might pull through.'

She lifted her face, her mouth turned square and her eyes squinted and he knew she was making a huge effort to hold back tears. He couldn't resist drawing her closer and she sank into him, warm and unresisting, needing his support, which he gave gladly.

The bulge of her baby pressed against him and he felt an instant rush of overwhelming tenderness for her. For her, for her baby...even for the pathetic little bird she cared so much about.

She clung to him, burrowing her face into his shoulder. He gave in to the impulse to thread his fingers through her shiny black hair. It was as silky and soft as he knew it would be and slipped through his fingers like glossy satin ribbons.

He touched her cheek and her skin was as soft as wattle blossoms. He knew the rest of her was soft, too. Soft and warm and sweet and womanly and sexy as hell and...

She lifted her head and looked into his eyes and he could see the full force of her emotions. And he knew it was totally inappropriate, but all he could think of was taking her back to his room right then, and kissing her, losing himself in her.

'Poor Oscar,' he heard her say and he came zinging back to reality. 'I know I'm being pathetic about him,' she said, 'but he's the only pet I've ever owned. He's the only family I have. I don't know if I'll be able to bear it if he dies.'

He dropped his hands to his sides and tried to concentrate on her words. Tried not to think about sex.

'Maybe he's elderly. Maybe it's his time,' he suggested helplessly.

Shaking her head, she walked away from him and slumped into a chair at the kitchen table.

'Perhaps you should give in and have a little cry,' he suggested.

She shook her head. 'I can't. I mustn't.'

Puzzled, he pulled out another chair and sat opposite her. 'Hey, you're a woman. You're allowed to cry.'

Her chin lifted and she glared at him. 'That's sexist rubbish.'

Of course. This was Stella the feminist scientist—not one of his sisters. 'OK, I'll try again. You're very upset. Crying is supposed to help release your emotions.'

'But I can't cry,' she whispered.

They were looking straight into each other's eyes again and he saw a vulnerability in her that completely contradicted the harshness of her claim. 'Stella,' he said, 'what do you mean? Don't you ever cry?'

'No.'

'Not ever?'

She drew in a deep, shuddering breath. 'I can't possibly cry for a sick bird when I—I didn't even cry when my mother died.'

Fine hairs rose on the back of his neck as he recognised

the significance of this moment. This was the taboo subject. Her mother.

Cautiously, he asked, 'When did your mother die?'

She stiffened.

'Were you very young?'

'I—I was fifteen.'

Only fifteen. 'And, at fifteen, you had already learned to hold back your tears?'

She didn't answer and he could picture the teenage Stella with her chin up, her shoulders back and her eyes glinting fiercely.

'You promised to tell me about your family sometime,' he reminded her gently.

She shook her head wearily. 'You might hate me if I do.'

'Hate you?' He was truly shocked.

'Your family are so perfect.' She patted her stomach and her voice was edged with bitterness as she said, 'Ruby will be inheriting thoroughbred genes from your side.'

'But Stella, what about your contribution? Your baby will have a mother who's a very clever scientist.'

'And a grandmother who was an alcoholic and a prostitute!'

She flung the words at him harshly, so harshly he almost flinched. But he knew that was what she expected. This was what she'd been trying to hide from him for so long.

Determined to show no sign of shock, he asked, 'So…did you live with your mother?'

'Now and again. In between a string of foster homes. She could never keep me for very long.'

'But she tried?'

'Oh, yes. She tried. Over and over.' She pressed her lips together and took a deep breath through her nose. 'I guess the maternal instincts were there, but the grog got in the way.'

'Well, you might have inherited her instincts. There's every chance you'll be a fantastic mother.'

She shook her head. 'I doubt it. Anyway, now you know why it's best that I leave my baby with you.'

This was another shock. 'You mean your real reason for going away is because you have no faith in yourself as a mother? It's not just the job in London?'

Stella covered her face with her hands. 'There are a thousand reasons why I'm going.'

He was tempted to suggest that running away never solved problems, but he suspected that it wouldn't be wise to start lecturing her right now when she'd waited so long to take him into her confidence. 'What about your father?'

Her lip curled. 'The news gets better and better. I know absolutely zilch about my father. Not even his name.' She looked impossibly tense as if she was waiting for his re-action to fall on her like a heavy blow. 'On my birth cer-tificate it says, "Father Unknown".'

'That's tough.'

'Aren't you glad you know all this?'

What he knew was that he wanted to hold her again.

Her eyes narrowed. 'What would Senator Roper think of this news?'

'What he thinks is irrelevant.'

'Won't he be horrified that his grandchild has such a black pedigree?'

'Stella, in the outback we judge people by how they live day to day. When you're dealing with an unforgiving land, what counts is what a man does now. Today. The past no longer matters. Right now I'm looking at you and I'm seeing a very clever woman, who's achieved a great deal on her own, without any family support. That takes guts.'

She smiled wanly, reached over and patted his hand. 'Thanks.' After a pause, she added, 'I want Scott's baby to experience your kind of family. Not mine. Yours is such a jolly perfect family—stable, salt of the earth and all that.'

'I can't imagine how hard it must be to have no idea who your father is.'

Her face crumpled and for a moment he thought that this time she would let a tear or two fall. But no. She took another deep breath and fixed him with a steady gaze. 'That's why you must tell Ruby all about Scott. I want her to know everything about her father. What a great guy he was.'

'Yeah.' His throat felt rough and choked. 'You—you can count on that.'

'The only thing my mother ever told me about my father was that he was a university professor. I was born when she was quite young—before she went downhill so to speak.'

'Well, there you go!' Callum exclaimed. 'A professor. At least you know where all those brains come from.'

'When I was at university, I used to look at all the professors and try to guess if my father was one of them. I would think that I could be sitting in his lectures—right under his nose—and he would never know about me. There was one professor of physics I really liked. He was incredibly clever and kind and he cracked jokes that were actually funny.' Her mouth tilted. 'I used to pretend he was my father.'

'You never know. I suppose there's a small chance that he might have been. You could probably try to find out if you wanted to.'

She shook her head. 'I wouldn't want to lay that kind of shock at his feet. Anyhow, I could never imagine him getting together with Marlene.'

'Was that your mother's name?'

'Yeah.'

'Did she look like you?'

Stella shrugged. 'A bit.' Then she gave a self-deprecating little laugh. 'A lot.'

Callum had no problems imaging a kind, clever guy wanting to get together with a woman who looked like Stella.

'I don't like to think about either of my parents very often.'

So is that why you're running away? Do you want your baby to grow up without the baggage of either of her parents? The questions hovered in his mind, but this wasn't the right moment to ask them. Not when she was feeling so low.

Suddenly her head jerked up and she stared past him, her eyes wide and a blast of joy lit her features. 'Callum, look at Oscar!'

He turned to see the little bird hopping across the floor of the cage to peck at his tray of seed.

'He's eating!' she cried.

'Blow me down.'

She jumped up and hurried over to the cage. 'Do you think he's better?'

'It's got to be a good sign,' Callum said, coming to join her. And as he stood watching the hope and happiness linger in Stella's eyes, he wished to hell he could find a way to make her look at him that way.

CHAPTER TEN

STELLA thought she knew about weather, but experiencing steamy northern temperatures was quite different from recording them on a chart. As the weeks passed and her stomach grew rounder, the days grew hotter. She longed for the cool southerly winds that brought relief to hot days in Sydney, but she knew she hoped in vain.

It was even too hot for Callum to work. He'd spent several afternoons stretched on the sofa, reading through a pile of cattle industry journals with his shirt unbuttoned and wearing denim shorts rather than his usual jeans.

Oscar had recovered, thank God, but he'd given her such a terrible fright that she fussed over him more than ever. Today she'd placed a pedestal fan near his cage in the kitchen and now she was trying to find a comfortable spot for herself on the lounge carpet directly under the ceiling fan. She was dressed in a skimpy pink T-shirt-style smock and she knew she looked a mess.

Given the size of her tummy, she was quite certain she looked more like a giant strawberry than a human being. And because it was too hot to have her hair down, she'd scrunched it into a knot on top of her head, but fine bits of it kept escaping.

She was having another go at reading a book about childbirth. When the book had first arrived, she'd skimmed through it and hadn't liked what she'd found. Everything about giving birth had sounded way too gruesome and she'd filed the book away and had tried to put the whole subject out of her mind.

But now she was eight months' pregnant and the issue was becoming harder to ignore. Callum's mother and sisters had been asking her if she was preparing for natural childbirth. And on her regular trips to Mount Isa, the midwife at the hospital kept mentioning the benefits of breathing techniques, birthing positions and relaxation exercises.

Relaxation? They had to be joking.

She had just read an entire chapter of relaxation exercises and had tried them out and none of them seemed to work. Flipping back to the beginning, she puffed out her lips with a resigned sigh and decided she had better give it one more try.

Imagine you're floating on a huge fluffy cloud. You're sinking into it. Let it support you totally. Your whole body is relaxing. First your feet and legs let go, then your hips, your torso, your chest. Breathe in regularly and slowly.

A fly buzzed past her nose and settled on her foot. She tried to ignore it, but eventually she had to shake it away.

'Damn,' she muttered. And that was the end of her relaxation. She'd have to start on the fluffy cloud all over again.

Callum lowered his journal and looked at her. His gaze rested on her feet and she saw his frown.

'You don't paint your toenails any more.'

'No, I've given up.'

'Any particular reason?'

'A very simple one, Callum. I can't.'

His frown deepened. 'Why not? Have you run out of paint?'

She rolled her eyes. Men could be so dense. 'Haven't you noticed? There's an enormous bump where my waist used to be, which means I can't reach my toes. Half the time I can't even see them.'

He dropped the magazine and sat up, swinging his long legs over the edge of the sofa. His unbuttoned shirt fell open, offering her a tempting view of his very masculine chest with its nice shadowing of dark hair.

He smiled. 'We'll have to do something about this. Stella without toenail polish is like—like the Mona Lisa without her smile, the Statue of Liberty without her lamp—'

'It's not that big a deal.'

His eyes widened and it was hard to tell if he was making fun of her or deadly serious. 'I mean it, Stella. We can't have you going around with your toenails bare. Not that there's anything wrong with your nails, but they should be coloured. They're an important part of who you are.'

'You really think so?'

'Too right.'

She wanted to give him a hug, but that would be silly since she and Callum were avoiding that kind of closeness. But how had he guessed that her painted toenails were important to her, like a badge of courage? How did he know that she'd hated not being able to reach them any more?

Ever since she'd been little when one of her foster mothers had told her that her face was plain but she had pretty feet, she'd been pathetically vain about her feet.

Now an unexpected glow warmed her insides. Callum understood. He cared.

'Would you like me to paint them for you?' he asked.

She hid her pleased surprise behind a mocking chuckle. 'I'd like to see you try.'

His eyebrows rose. 'You don't think I could do it?'

'I can't imagine it.'

He stood up and towered above her and his smile broadened to a grin. 'I'm not going to let a slight like that go unchallenged, young lady. Prepare to have your toenails painted by an expert.'

Oh, heavens, he was serious. Suddenly she pictured his big brown hands holding her feet. 'I was joking,' she cried. 'I don't need them painted.'

'Yes, you do. Now, don't get up. Tell me where you keep all the toenail stuff.'

'Um…' Stella gulped. This was silly. She and Callum didn't do this kind of thing. It was too—too intimate.

'If you don't tell me, I'll just hunt around in your bathroom till I find what I need,' he said.

Secretly thrilled, she gave in. 'There's a blue and silver striped bag in the cupboard on the left.'

'I'll be right back.'

He was gone before she could voice a protest, and back before she'd thought up an excuse. By the time he was kneeling on the carpet beside her, with his shirt still undone and all that naked chest exposed, her brain was going into meltdown. Heavens! She needed to think of a smart retort that would send him away again.

She and Callum avoided situations like this. It was as if they'd tacitly agreed that anything remotely touchy-feely was no-go territory. For Stella's part, she still feared the powerful attraction she felt for him. She feared losing control and she suspected that, if Callum tempted her, there was every chance her control would scatter to the winds.

For weeks now, an uncomfortable chemistry had been mounting between them. If they were sensible—if they kept their distance—it stayed at an only-just-bearable low simmer.

So far they'd been sensible.

So what on earth did Callum think he was doing? How could he spoil it all now by playing with her feet? Maybe he thought her feet were a safe extremity but, as far as Stella was concerned, having Callum touch any part of her body posed a problem.

He unzipped the pack and pulled out several bottles of nail polish. 'What colour would you like? Blue?'

'Pale pink would be safer. If you muck it up, it won't be so noticeable.'

'If I muck it up!' He managed to look affronted. 'I'd appreciate a little more faith, woman. If I can paint a machinery shed, I can paint a toenail.' He selected a bottle of Baby Blush. 'This one do?'

She nodded.

'Are you comfortable?'

Before she could answer, he dragged an armchair closer and piled a mountain of cushions between her back and the chair.

'That's great. Thanks.'

'OK. Let's see.' He settled comfortably in front of her and held her foot between his legs and she tried not to look at his chest, or the latent power in his bare thighs, or—*gulp*—the very masculine shape that strained against the centre seam of his denim shorts.

'Now, what do I have to do?' he asked. 'Do I need to sand your nails back? Is there an undercoat that goes on first?'

'Just a coat of colour will be fine,' she said breathlessly.

Carefully, he shook the little pot of polish, then slowly unscrewed the lid and extracted the tiny brush.

Stella smiled as she watched the intense concentration

on his face as he wiped excess polish from the brush and began to apply paint to the nail of her big toe with the serious attention of a heart surgeon. He looked so dreadfully conscientious, she wanted to giggle.

'Callum, you can lighten up on this. It's not as if anyone else is going to see my feet. *I* only glimpse them occasionally these days.'

He didn't answer, didn't even acknowledge that he'd heard her, as he drew a final stripe of colour neatly over the nail. Bending his head, he blew gently on her toe and Stella felt so suddenly hot, she knew she must be blushing. He looked at the next toe and frowned.

'There's a toe separator in the bag,' she told him.

'A toe separator,' he murmured, but he didn't seem too interested in hunting for it. Instead of rummaging through her bag, he put the brush back into the pot, re-screwed the cap, blew on her nail once again and then ran his finger down the little valley between her big toe and the next.

What was he doing?

His eyes were downcast, concentrating on her foot, so she couldn't see his expression. And perhaps it was just as well he wasn't looking at her face. He might see how hot and bothered she was feeling. 'That toe will be dry. You can keep on going.'

He acted as if he hadn't heard her and began to trace his fingers with teasing slowness between the rest of her toes.

'Callum,' she whispered.

'Just separating them.' He looked up. Their gazes locked and her insides went into free fall when she saw the languid burning in his eyes.

'You're supposed to be painting my nails, not giving me a foot massage.'

'Patience,' he murmured. But instead of returning to the

task, he trailed his hand down the sole of her foot. Her heart began to clatter as he cupped her heel in the palm of one hand while he rubbed gentle circles around the tip of each toe. 'Don't you like this?'

Oh, help! This shouldn't be happening. Not with Callum. He shouldn't be touching her like this. It felt so incredible. Each touch seemed to reach deep inside her. Too deep. Too much. 'I hate it,' she whispered.

'Liar.' He lowered his mouth and kissed the inner curve of her arch.

Flaming rivers rippled under her skin and spread like a runaway fire from her toes, up her legs and along the insides of her thighs until they pooled low and urgent inside her. *She mustn't moan.* 'What—what do you think you're doing?'

His smile was both shy and wild and it definitely spelled danger. 'I don't know. What do you think I'm doing?'

Trying to seduce me? With total success! 'Maybe you have heatstroke?'

'Can't be heatstroke. Feels too good.' He was kissing her toes. No, not just kissing them—he was running his tongue over their sensitive tips. And it felt—

Stella was coming undone. Slowly, quickly, she wasn't sure. The lazy afternoon seemed to be spinning away as her sense of time and place melted into *now* and *this*.

He lowered one foot and took up the other and his smile lost any trace of shyness as he held her foot against his thigh.

'Callum, we shouldn't be—' she cried, but even as she said it she was pushing her foot boldly forward, sliding it out of his hand until she touched him. She couldn't help herself. She had to touch him. Through his shorts. *Right there!*

He stilled. 'Stella, what do you think you're doing?'

'I don't know,' she whispered, feeling too hot, too gone to think. All she wanted was to feel. To feel Callum at last.

She ran daring toes over the tough cotton of his shorts, and the fever inside her roared as she felt his response surge hard beneath her foot. She heard her own gasps—heard his groan.

And next minute, he was pulling her down beside him on the carpet. Cushions scattered and his mouth turned savage and hungry.

It was terrifying yet wonderful! They'd waited too long for this. Far too long. Too many days, weeks, months of not touching. Now, every good intention exploded and scattered all around them.

Callum kissed her mouth and she adored the feel and the taste of him, loved the deep thrust of his tongue, so male and wonderfully intimate. So good. So right.

She ran excited fingers through the hair on his chest and shivered with pleasure as he kissed her neck. When his mouth found her breasts through the thin cotton of her dress, she couldn't hold back soft moans as she arched and yearned for more. Oh, yes! Yes!

He whispered her name and it had never sounded so lovely, so sexy.

She could tell he was being careful not to hurt her baby, but their bodies strained for the closest possible contact.

'We mustn't,' she protested weakly.

'I know. I know.'

'But I want you,' she cried. And she did. There had never been a time when she'd felt such wanting. She had never felt like this with Scott. Never. Now she accepted the truth that she'd always wanted this man.

'Oh, God, Stella.'

They were on fire. It was far too late to pull back.

But surely they couldn't take the last plunging leap into complete intimacy?

'Just let me touch you, Stella.'

'Oh, yes, Callum!'

Yes! She was losing control. The overwhelming urgency in her demanded release. No more protests. No more words. Too late to fear this. All she wanted was to surrender.

His impatient mouth covered hers again and, pushing her clothing aside, his hand grew more daring.

His caresses became more loving, each touch an intimate gift. And then she was lost, disintegrating in a wild, glorious star burst.

Lifting damp strands of hair away from her cheek, Callum tucked them behind her ear and watched as she opened her beautiful eyes. Eyes that shimmered with such strong emotion that his heart leapt like a high-vaulting stallion.

He almost said something crazy. A dead give-away like, *I think I love you.* But memories of that first time in Sydney—that other time when their strong attraction had flared out of control—kept him quiet. He had scared her off then.

Now, despite the self-conscious shyness in her eyes, she was smiling up at him. 'If that's how you paint toenails— you must be amazing—in—in bed.'

He smiled. 'With you I'd win medals.'

She blushed and he watched as her smile turned wistful and dreamy. Suddenly she looked very young and vulnerable and guilt sent his heart plummeting. Hell! She'd been trusting him to keep his promise that there would be no intimacy in their marriage. 'But we can't find out, Stella, can we?'

Her smile vanished. 'No, of course not.'

Their glances slid away and he sat very still beside her on the carpet with his hands locked around his bent knees. His guilty thoughts seemed to hover unspoken in the steamy room and the only sound was Mac's panting as he lay sprawled in the hallway leading out to the veranda.

Stella was the first to move. She propped herself up on one elbow and studied Callum with a typically level Stella-style gaze. 'You broke your promise.'

He nodded and grimaced. 'I did. I'm sorry.' What else could he say? If he tried to explain his actions, he would end up telling her how he really felt about her and that could scare her off completely.

When she made no response, he cleared his throat. 'About those toenails.'

'What about them?'

'I—I still want to paint them. I've become used to see-ing all those different colours trotting around the place.'

Awkwardly, she pushed herself higher until she was sit-ting cross-legged on the carpet. 'Callum, is this your way of saying let's not talk about what just happened?'

His airways seemed to contract. 'No. We can talk about it.'

'Do you think it was a mistake?'

'Well, I guess it was, but it was my mistake, not yours.'

She dropped her gaze. 'It doesn't change anything, does it?'

'How do you mean?'

The colour in her cheeks deepened. 'What I mean is— it was just sparks, wasn't it? Just chemistry? Nothing deep and meaningful.'

Fear flickered in her eyes and a stab of regret speared his heart. What a dent to the ego this girl was. It was just as he'd feared. The last thing Stella Lassiter wanted was a deep and meaningful relationship with Scott Roper's brother.

He shook his head slowly. 'Don't worry, Stella. I'm sure what just happened was simply the result of a healthy man and a woman spending too much time alone together in the bush.'

Nervously, she chewed at her lip and pulled at a loose thread in the carpet. 'We'd really stuff things up if we take this any further.'

He tried for a grin, but it faltered. 'Of course.'

'You made it very clear about this marriage and legalities—'

'Yeah. From a legal point of view, things would be more complicated if we consummate the marriage.'

She pulled harder on the thread until it began to unravel. 'I hope you don't think I'd try to get my hands on a share of Birralee.'

Callum stared at her. 'That sounded like a round about way of saying you want to have sex with me.'

Her face turned bright red and she almost choked on her shocked gasp. 'No! Heavens, no! Of course, I didn't mean—'

'OK, OK!' He jumped in quickly before she expanded her protest into a five-minute speech. 'Look, I'm not worried that you're going to start demanding a share of this property. I'm just trying to make things easier for everyone concerned when you—when you come back from London.'

The thread in her hand snapped.

His heart stilled. 'You still want to go away, don't you?'

'I—think so,' she whispered.

A small boulder seemed to wedge itself in his throat. 'You're not sure?'

She sighed and gave her middle a pat. 'These days I can't seem to think beyond this little one's arrival.'

'That's—that's understandable.'

He laid his hand beside hers on her stomach. It was so very round and tight and burgeoning with life. He felt the baby move. The kick was surprisingly strong. He could feel the outline of the little foot and he could picture the baby curled safely inside Stella's womb, ready and eager to escape into the world. He was gripped by a sudden urge to see it, to hold it in his arms. 'It won't be long now,' he said gently.

There was a sudden flash of panic in her eyes. Her whole body seemed to sag and her attention darted to the book she'd been reading. 'Don't remind me,' she whispered.

'Are you scared?'

'Too right.'

He picked the book up. 'What about all this reading you've been doing? Hasn't it been any help?'

She shrugged.

'I'm sure you'll be OK, Stell. You're young and healthy and I've promised to make sure you fly into Mount Isa in plenty of time.'

'I know. But—oh, Callum. There's more to having a baby than arriving at the hospital in time. I don't know if I can bear the thought of all that pain. I think I'm going to be queen of the wimps.'

'You'll be OK. You're tough.'

She compressed her lips and closed her eyes as if she was holding back tears. 'It's all bluff. Deep down I'm a quivering coward.'

He saw the unmistakable tension in her and remembered her fears about motherhood. He'd seen plenty of animals in labour and had a fair idea how fear could make the process so much more difficult.

Suddenly he was afraid for her. Given her circumstances, there was a good chance she would fight against giving birth rather than working with it. That could mean she would have a very hard time.

He looked at the book in his hands. 'How about I read up on all this childbirth stuff, too? Maybe I could help somehow—be your coach.'

The wash of relief in her face was amazing. Her smile couldn't have been warmer if he'd offered to buy her the moon and the stars. 'Would you really do that?'

His heart quaked at the thought of seeing her suffer, but he'd leap tall buildings in a single bound if it made her look at him that way. 'Yeah. I'll be there if you want me to.'

'Oh, Callum,' she cried and she threw herself forward, wrapping her arms around him. 'That would be so wonderful. I know I could manage if you were there.'

It was hard to believe this was Stella. Stella the tough girl. The feminist scientist. She was looking at him with eyes that were glowing with trust and she was literally begging him to be her knight in shining armour.

And he couldn't resist cupping her face in his hands and dipping his mouth to hers. He had to taste again the sweet, moist lushness of her parted lips. 'I'll be there,' he murmured. 'We'll be a great team.'

'Promise?'

'I promise.'

'What if you're away on a muster or something when I go into labour?'

He kissed the tip of her nose, and stroked her soft lower lip with his thumb. 'We've each got a satellite phone. I'll keep mine with me all the time and, come hell or high water, I'll be there with you, Stella. I promise.'

Stella knew Callum was a man of his word, but she was truly surprised by how seriously he approached the preparation for her labour. After two weeks with him as her personal childbirth coach, she was beginning to feel like an athlete training for a big race.

He read every book she'd bought and each evening he made her practise the relaxation exercises and the various breathing techniques over and over until he was satisfied that she was totally familiar with them.

But the best part was how good she felt just knowing that he was going to be there in the delivery room with her, checking her breathing, helping her to relax, cheering her on to the finish line.

The electric tension still zapped between them, but now that they'd discussed it they could deal with it more easily. At least that was what Stella tried to tell herself. But, in reality, she was finding it harder than ever to ignore the way she felt about Callum.

The way she felt about leaving him! The paperwork from the British television network had been forwarded from Sydney confirming what she'd known all along: she was expected to arrive in London in eight weeks' time.

Eight weeks! It was as if she'd been running merrily along through an obstacle course, pretending that because she couldn't see the hurdles they weren't there. Now she'd run smack bang into the big one.

'What's that?' Callum asked when he saw the official-looking yellow envelope.

'Oh, just some forms I have to fill out.'

Vertical creases ran between his brows. 'So this is it, the final commitment?'

'Yes.' Suddenly she could hardly breathe.

Callum stood stock still before her and she saw his hands clench tightly against his sides. He looked so unexpectedly white and *sick*, Stella's heart boomed like a bass drum.

And in a flash she knew exactly how she felt about going. If he told her not to sign the papers, she would stay here. All he had to do was say that he needed her.

She could keep her baby and she could keep him. Was it selfish to want them both? Her heart twisted so sharply it was hard to think straight. Surely if she stayed here she could make herself useful. With a background in environmental studies there were many ways she could adapt her knowledge to assist a cattleman.

Oh, Lord, should I tell him that?

Her mouth opened, the words quivering on her lips, but suddenly Callum gave a shake as if he were ridding himself of an unwanted thought. 'You'd better get everything signed, sealed and delivered straight away,' he said. 'In case you have to dash off to hospital. You'd never forgive yourself if you forgot to post important stuff like that.'

She felt the blast of disappointment like a slap in the face. He sounded so matter-of-fact. Perhaps she'd imagined that fleeting moment when he looked ill at the thought of her leaving?

'I suppose I should send them straight back.' She couldn't hold back a sigh.

'You wouldn't want to mess things up at this stage.'

'No.'

Strange how truly dreadful she felt. Lately she'd found it more and more difficult to dredge up excitement about the job overseas. Other dreams kept nudging it aside. Dreams of the little human being who was sharing her body. A little pink and white baby. Someone who called her Mummy.

When she tried to picture herself as part of a fascinating team of scientists and television people working their way around European coastlines, she kept seeing the red earth and blue skies of the outback. And the recognition of colleagues didn't seem nearly as important now as the smiling approval of honey-brown eyes.

But of course, Callum was right.

She couldn't give up on London now and she had no right to hold him to this marriage. It would be unfair after he'd given up so much for her to suddenly change her mind and plead with him to let her stay. If he'd wanted her to stay, he would have admitted it weeks ago, after they'd been so intimate.

After dinner, she filled in the forms, signed them and slipped them into a clean envelope ready for the mail truck in the morning.

Callum saw the envelope sitting ready, but made no further comment. Instead he told her, 'There's a section of fence down near the Paroo gorge. I'm rather unhappy about it. Some of the cattle have already found their way through it and if they get right down into that really wild country, I'll have hell's own job getting them out again.'

'So you want to go out there tomorrow?'

'I should muster those strays back through the fence. But it's further away from base than I like to go these days.'

Stella tried to squash a little spurt of panic. 'Go, Callum. The baby isn't due for another two weeks and apparently first babies are nearly always late.'

His eyes were dark with concern. 'You're sure you'll be OK?'

'Of course. I can always get you on the satellite phone if I have to, but I haven't felt the faintest twinge.'

'I'll be as quick as I can.'

He left in the four-wheel drive straight after breakfast, taking Nugget and Cleo, two of the station's working dogs and his stallion, Blackjack, in a trailer. Mac stayed behind at the homestead.

'To keep you company,' Callum told Stella. 'Don't mention the word muster in his hearing or he'll twig that we've gone without him and he'll spend the whole morning whining.'

When he reached the section of broken fence, he parked the vehicle and continued on horseback, crossing a wide and sandy river-bed. Gums grew in the river-bed and in a narrow strip along each bank. On the far side he reached the rough scrub where the cattle were most likely to have strayed.

There was a good chance the herd had been joined by some cleanskins—wild cattle that had never seen a branding iron, a drench gun or an ear tag. Some might never have seen a human.

Mustering on his own wasn't wise, but with Stella's time drawing so close he didn't want to delay things by waiting till one of his neighbours was free to lend a hand.

He held the reins lightly in one hand, while with the other he tugged at his akubra, pulling it low over his eyes as protection from the savage brilliance of the sun.

In the past, he'd always found that he could think more clearly when he was riding, but this morning, as he trailed through the scrub, he didn't want to think, didn't want to remember how he'd felt last night when he'd seen the large official envelope addressed to Stella. Didn't want to think about how he felt about her, how bone-deep lonely he would be when she was gone.

He kept his eyes peeled looking for colour, for the movement that would betray the presence of the herd but, in spite of his concentration, thoughts of Stella elbowed their way back into his head.

He'd always maintained that a man in the bush developed a gut instinct for recognising a certain rightness about some things and as he rode this morning, taking his fill of the landscape he loved, the more he thought, the more he became absolutely, no-doubt-about-it dead certain that he knew what was right for him—and for Stella, the baby, Mac, even Oscar, damn it.

They should all be together at Birralee. For ever.

He'd been crazy to try to pretend things should be any other way.

No matter how hard he tried to shake the conviction, it wouldn't budge. Hell, it was the truth and he had to tell Stella. It was time to wear his heart on his sleeve. To be honest and up front.

She could go to London if she had to, but then she had to come back to him. *Soon as the time's up, I'll get her. Even if I have to track her down in some Norwegian fjord, I'm going to get her and bring her back.*

With that decision made, his heart felt lighter. Just as soon as he'd found these flaming cattle, he'd tell her.

Topping a slight rise, he saw the herd scattered below. He and the dogs moved in quickly. Nugget, the speedier animal, expertly covered the far wing of the herd while Cleo took the other flank and Callum, yelling fiercely and cracking his whip, came at them from behind.

Years of experience had taught him how to read cattle and he was ready for the cantankerous scrub bull when it charged. With an angry roar and a loud crack of his stock whip, he turned it from its frenzied dash towards the heavy timber to his right and soon it was back in with the herd, not happy, but more subdued.

Confident that the dogs could handle the mob, he made

a quick check of the gullies to the left. There were stragglers there, too. Digging in his heels, he pushed Blackjack down the rocky shale, anxious to get the job over, urging him further down the steep gully, closer to the rogue beasts.

Neither he nor Blackjack saw the melon hole. Without warning, he felt the horse lose balance beneath him. He fought to stay in the saddle, but next moment his valiant, sturdy stallion was pitching forward and Callum was thrown.

CHAPTER ELEVEN

IT WAS a bad fall. As Callum hit the ground, his right foot caught in the stirrup and he felt the sharp-shooting agony of his ankle being wrenched apart. Damn it to hell! He'd broken bones.

Rocky shale dug into his back and he gritted his teeth as he lay there, fighting back pain while he waited for the world to stop spinning and his vision to clear.

Eventually he could turn his head. Squinting against the cruel sun that blazed directly overhead, he made out the dark shape of Blackjack standing nearby. The startled animal was shaking. But at least he hadn't bolted and he didn't look hurt. That was a relief.

Callum knew what he had to do. There was no time to examine his injury. He had to move very quickly, before the ankle went cold and shock set in. Swallowing a groan, he edged himself up the slope. Just a little closer and with a clumsy lurch, he was able to reach for the dangling reins.

It was only sheer strength of will that got him to his feet. Just for a moment he had to take his weight on his busted leg while he clung to the saddle and yelled curses as he raised his good foot into the stirrups.

Waves of dizziness claimed him as he slumped forward over the saddle. Then, grimacing with the effort, he unbuttoned his shirt pocket and extracted his phone. He hated the thought of ringing Stella and telling her what had happened, but it had to be done.

But as soon as he depressed the buttons, he realised the

phone was dead. He checked the batteries, tried again. Still
no luck. Must have damaged it during the fall.

He swore, knowing there was nothing for it but to get
himself home.

A flick from the reins sent Blackjack heading back up
the slope in the direction of the vehicle. On the ridge ahead
of him, he could see the stragglers at the end of the mob.
The dogs were still working them, leading them back to
the fence, but there was no way he could mend the broken
panel today, so the cattle would soon be back. A morning's
effort wasted.

Molten blasts of pain were shooting through his ankle
by the time the horse came to a halt next to the truck. It
was hard to keep thinking and moving with so much discomfort, but somehow he managed to dismount.

But getting Blackjack back into the trailer was beyond
him. Breathing hard, he leaned against the side of the
truck, loosened the girth straps and let the saddle drop to
the ground, then he slapped his hand against the stallion's
rump and sent him to find his own way home.

By crikey, his leg was bad. Cursing bad. Callum let fly
with another loud volley of swearing as he levered himself
up into the truck. Once he was behind the steering wheel,
he had to sit there for several minutes, taking big breaths,
trying to beat the pain. Eventually, he whistled the dogs
and they leapt into the ute's tray back.

OK. He wiped the sweat from his face with his shirt
sleeve. Driving with his left foot on the accelerator was
going to be tricky, but he had to do it. Had to get home
as soon as he could.

A couple of times on the long trip back, shadowy darkness threatened to consume him and he thought he might
lose consciousness. His energy seemed to be draining away
and he wasn't sure how he kept the truck going, how he

kept the steering wheel steady, how he kept his eyes
open...

It seemed like twenty years before he reached Birralee,
and by then he knew he couldn't move. All he could do
was sit with his hand on the horn, waiting for Stella.

The long, drawn out blast of the truck's horn terrified
Stella. Mac began barking immediately, terrifying her even
more as she rushed to the window. It was Callum's truck.
What on earth? What was wrong?

As quickly as her rotund shape would allow, she raced
after Mac, through the house, across the veranda, down the
steps and over the sloping paddock to the truck.

'Callum, what is it? Oh, my God, what's happened?'

He was slumped over the steering wheel and she saw
dried blood on his forehead. *Was he dead?* Her heart
seemed to crash against the wall of her chest and she
thought it might burst through as she wrenched the driver's
door open. 'Callum!' she screamed.

*Oh, God, no! Callum! He couldn't be dead. Not like
Scott. No, No!*

'Callum!'

He lifted his head and his face was deathly white as he
peered at her. 'Came off my horse.'

'Oh, heavens—' A sob disrupted the already ragged
rhythm of her breathing and she gulped as she tried to draw
in a breath. 'Where—where are you hurt?'

'Busted my leg.'

'What about your head?'

'Think it's OK.' He looked at her groggily. 'Stell, I want
to talk to you.'

'What about?'

''bout us.'

'Bad timing,' she whispered. 'Don't try to talk now.

Let's think about how we can get you out of there. Can you lean on me?'

'Don't even think about it—too heavy for you.'

'You need a doctor.'

''Fraid so.'

'Right.' She was calming down, forcing herself to think straight. She could do this. She wasn't about to cave in. She could be tough. Hadn't she already planned for medical emergencies like this? Just last week she'd programmed the number for the Flying Doctor into the phone and she'd written Birralee's latitude and longitude onto a wall chart in the office so she could give the doctor their precise location. 'Stay there, Callum. I'll be right back.'

'Not going anywhere.'

Again she was flying over the grass, but now, instead of feeling sheer terror, she felt purposeful. Frightened but *almost* composed. One press of the correct button and her call was connected straight to the flying doctor base. The news was good. There was a plane in their vicinity and it could be with them soon.

Next she found a blanket to keep Callum warm, and once she had that tucked around him she fled back to the kitchen to make him a Thermos of tea. Back down the steps and across the paddock.

As she lifted the strong, sweet brew to his lips, he muttered, 'You'll wear yourself out, Stell. I'm OK, don't fuss over me.'

'I like fussing over you.' He looked awful—his skin was pasty and caked with dust, sweat and dried blood. His eyes were bleary and bloodshot, his lips as colourless as rain.

'I want to talk to you.'

'Not now, Callum. Shut up and drink.'

'Since when did you get so bossy?'

'Since you showed signs of suffering from shock. At least the doctor's on his way.'

'He'll probably want to take me into Mount Isa.'

'Then, I'm coming, too. You can talk to me when we're safely on the plane.'

He groaned. 'Sorry about this. I've really stuffed up!'

'Of course you haven't. Now, listen, my hospital bag's already packed, but I'm going back to the house to pack a few things for you. And I'll ring the neighbours on Drayton Downs.'

'Good idea.'

'I'll ask them to take the dogs and Oscar over to their place.'

He nodded and grimaced, and his face leached whiter than ever.

'Oh, Callum, you poor darling.' She kissed his cold cheek. 'I feel bad about leaving you even to make another phone call.'

She couldn't be sure what deep emotion she saw in his dark gaze, then he closed his eyes. 'I'll be fine.'

By the time she had Callum's bag packed and had contacted the neighbours, the flying doctor's plane was already landing. He and the nurse hurried over the paddock. They were calm, friendly and competent, although they looked a little startled when they saw Stella's advanced state of pregnancy.

'I'm not the patient,' she told them as she led them behind the homestead to Callum in the truck. 'At least, not yet.'

In no time they had Callum out of the vehicle and were examining his ankle.

'We'll need X-rays,' the doctor told her. He gave Callum an injection for the pain. 'OK, mate. Let's immobilise this leg then we can get you back to town and patched up.'

Stella was glad she'd been prepared for her own trip to hospital. Everything was happening so quickly. In no time, they were carrying Callum on a stretcher to the small plane while she followed with the bags.

The take-off was smooth and soon Birralee homestead looked like a tiny matchbox way below them. The nurse was happy for Stella to sit beside Callum, holding his hand. Not that he noticed. He was so heavily sedated he wasn't aware of her presence.

'Don't you dare die,' she whispered, squeezing his hand tight. She felt frozen inside. The doctor had muttered something about the possibility of internal injuries. Callum couldn't die. He mustn't. He was too special, too kind, too loving…

Touching shaking fingers to the rough curls tumbling over his forehead, she felt a painful uncoiling of emotion. She gazed at the features she'd come to know so well and felt agony… It was as if a powerful emotion was being dragged to the surface from way deep inside her…from a place she'd kept locked up tightly since childhood.

The force of it was shaking her.

Oh, heavens! She'd tried to resist this! But she'd always known from the first night they'd met, that Callum had the power to make her feel this kind of out-of-control flooding of emotion.

As a little girl, she'd felt like this about her mother, Marlene, and she'd been hurt, time and again.

But Callum? She'd tried to resist his kisses, his kindness. Had he won? Lying there, completely unconscious, had he reached in and touched that place deep inside her where body meets soul?

'Callum,' she whispered, ignoring the nurse sitting quietly to one side. 'You mustn't die. Not you, too.' She bit back a sob. She mustn't cry. She mustn't. 'I think I might be in love with you. Really in love. I think Ruby and I might need you. Oh, Callum, I need to talk to you about it.'

Suddenly she remembered that he'd wanted to tell her something. Perhaps she should have listened, but at the time she'd been too frightened to stop for a chat.

Now, she was more frightened than ever.

Margaret Roper was understandably upset to get a phone call from the hospital.

'Right now Callum's in the theatre having his ankle set,' Stella told her. 'There are no internal injuries, thank heavens, and the doctors are confident that he will heal without complications.'

'Poor Callum!' Margaret sighed. 'And how unfortunate for you, dear, with the baby due so soon. This is the last thing you need.'

'Don't worry about me. I'm fine,' Stella assured her. It was almost the truth. For the past half-hour, she'd been getting cramp-like twinges in her lower abdomen and they were scaring the hell out of her, but there was absolutely no point in alarming her mother-in-law when she was thousands of kilometres away in Canberra.

'Where will you stay tonight, Stella?'

'I've found a motel right near the hospital.'

'Good. Now, don't you wear yourself out with running back and forth after Callum. Would you like me to fly up? Maybe there's some way I could help.'

A sharper twinge took Stella by surprise.

'Are you all right, dear?'

'Yes.' She took a deep breath. 'Thanks for the offer, Margaret, but I'm sure we'll be just fine. But I'd better go now. I'll get an early night and ring you in the morning with an update.'

'We'd certainly appreciate that. Take care, dear.'

Stella replaced the receiver and gave a little moan as she sagged against the wall of the telephone booth. Ouch! The cramps were moving out of twinge range and into something definite and scary.

Just as the books had predicted, they were gaining momentum. Like an advancing menace. And every pain was taking her down a path that would ultimately lead her away from Callum for ever. Away from Callum and her baby.

As the pain eased, she straightened and stepped out into the hospital corridor. She wondered if Margaret Roper would still call her dear after she'd run out on Callum.

Fat chance.

Callum was angry. He'd been kept sedated for most of the night and it was the early hours of the morning before he woke properly.

'Where's Stella?' he bellowed to the first unfortunate nurse who ventured near his hospital bed.

She frowned. 'I beg your pardon?'

'Where's the woman who came with me? Mrs Roper. My—my wife.' He'd used that word so rarely it still felt both strange and wonderful.

'The pregnant woman?'

'That's the one.'

'I think someone said she's over in the maternity wing.'

His throat contracted. 'What's she doing there?'

She favoured him with a smug smile. 'Having a baby I should think.'

'She can't be!' he shouted. 'It's not due for another twelve days.

'Shh, Mr Roper. You'll wake the other patients and you

shouldn't get yourself all het up. You've had a bad fracture. Last night you had surgery on your ankle and your lower leg has been set in a plaster cast. You need to take it easy.'

'It's only a busted leg and I've been taking it *too* flaming easy! You've kept me doped to the eyebrows for hours. Now I want to know about Stella.'

She let out a resigned sigh. 'Would you like me to check on her condition?'

'Of course.' After a moment he remembered to add, 'Please.'

As the nurse hurried away, his brain churned. Surely Stella wasn't in labour? He'd promised to be there. Oh, hell! She would be terrified.

Swinging her legs over the edge of the bed, Stella reached for her handbag on the bedside table.

'What are you doing?' asked the startled midwife.

'I've changed my mind,' she said. 'I've decided I don't want to have a baby today.'

'But my dear, you can't—'

Stella clenched her lips and did her best to ignore the new pain that threatened. 'Just watch me.' She tried to wriggle her hips forward so she could slide her ungainly body off the high bed, but the pain was beating her, building up too fast, too sharp, too strong! 'Oh-h-h!'

'Come on, dear. You're not going anywhere. You must try to relax.'

'I can't relax,' she wailed. 'I've never heard of—oh—oh!' She panted and groaned under another mountain of pain. 'There's no way anyone could relax through that,' she grunted when at last it was over. 'I'll come back tomorrow and try again then. Maybe I'll be feeling more ready for all this by tomorrow.'

'I'm sorry, Stella. You're having this baby today.'

'I can't!' she cried.

The midwife was looking determined. But Stella could be determined, too. 'I can't have this baby without Callum,' she said. 'He promised to be with me.'

'Callum? Is that your husband?'

'Yes. He was admitted yesterday with a broken ankle.'

The woman looked as if she was about to ask another question, but the phone on her desk began to ring. 'Just try to breathe through the pain,' she said then hurried away to answer it.

'Mr Roper, I've been talking to a midwife. Mrs Roper has been in the labour ward since midnight.'

'Midnight?' He looked at his watch. That was five hours ago! 'You've got to get me to her.'

'You can't possibly go in your condition.'

'You don't understand. She can't have this baby without me.'

The nurse smiled sweetly. 'Maybe she couldn't start it without you, but I can assure you that she can and she is having this baby on her own.'

'The hell she is. I insist you get me over there.'

The nurse laughed as if he'd cracked the joke of the century. 'Look, I've ordered a nice cup of tea and a snack for you. You must be starving. Why don't you settle back and try to relax? By the time you've eaten, you could be a daddy.'

'Forget the food,' he barked. 'I won't be eating it. I have to be there with her. I promised.'

The nurse's patience was wearing thin. She forgot to smile as she said, 'But that was before you had an accident.'

'Bull dust! Being a patient is a state of mind. I'm cured.

Now, if you won't help me, I'll find my own way to the labour ward.'

She placed a nervous hand on his arm. 'Don't be foolish. It's very sweet of you to want to be with your wife, but you have to think about your own condition, too. The surgeon left strict instructions, there's to be no weight on your leg. I don't have permission to move you just yet.'

'Then get permission.'

Her eyebrows rose and her voice sharpened. 'Rudeness is not going to help your wife. I can tell you one thing, Mr Roper,' she said as she hurried towards the door, 'until the surgeon does his rounds, you won't be going anywhere.'

We'll bloody see about that!

The breathing patterns and relaxation had seemed so easy when Stella had been sitting with Callum on the carpet in Birralee's lounge, but they were a darned sight harder now. Why, oh, why had her baby decided to come today when Callum couldn't help her?

She hadn't known such strong pain existed. Why hadn't anybody told her how bad this would be? Or that it went on and on and on. When the books talked about contractions building stronger and getting closer, they hadn't explained *how* strong or how close.

She was so tired of breathing and panting her way through each one. As for relaxing the rest of her body— that always came as an afterthought. So much for floating on fluffy clouds! What a joke! She'd never felt so *un*-relaxed, so uncomfortable in her life.

She was exhausted. And tense!

She needed a break.

And she didn't want her baby to be born now. It was imperative to sort things out with Callum first. Oh, help!

She drew in a deep, starting breath and began another cycle of breathing as more fiery pain consumed her.

'How much longer?' she groaned as the contraction faded at last.

'There, there,' came a voice that was meant to be soothing. 'You're doing just fine.'

'Maybe I need some drugs or something.'

The midwife examined her again. She beamed. 'You're almost fully dilated, Stella. Hang in there, sweetie. It really shouldn't be too much longer now.'

Her baby would be coming soon? Without Callum? The slam of panic almost flattened her. 'But I—I can't have a baby yet,' she moaned.

'Of course you can, dear.'

Another pain started. Lower, harder, hotter, fiercer. She felt warm liquid flow between her legs and spread on the sheet.

'There you go,' the midwife announced cheerily, 'your waters have broken. Things will really start to happen now.'

Oh, Lord! Stella knew that she shouldn't be so tense, but couldn't help it. She wanted Callum.

A sudden collision outside distracted her momentarily.

'Good heavens!' cried the midwife, but already Stella had stopped caring what was happening anywhere else. Right now, her body was the centre of the world.

With another loud bang, the double doors of the delivery room swung open. Through a haze of pain, Stella saw the midwife jumping out of the way as a wheelchair spun into the room and almost crashed into the bed. The chair's occupant was wearing a hospital gown and his leg was encased in plaster.

It couldn't be.

It was. It was Callum!

He was levering himself out of the chair.

The midwife was protesting. 'What do you think you're doing? How did you get in here?'

'Hijacked a wheelchair,' he muttered. 'I had to be here. This is my wife.'

'But you can't. You're supposed to be in—'

'Don't you start telling me what I can't do!'

There was silence and Stella could sense a battle of wills waging beside her.

Then suddenly she didn't care as another contraction gripped her. When it was over, she felt Callum's hands smoothing damp strands of hair away from her forehead and he pressed his lips to her cheek. 'Sorry I'm late, sweetheart,' he whispered. 'You're doing just great.'

'Can you stay?'

'You bet.' He ran a gentle hand down her arm. 'But, hey, you went ahead and started having this baby without me.'

'I didn't want to,' she whispered. 'I've been trying to stop it.'

'Don't do that, Stell. We need this baby out.'

'Do we?'

His warm eyes looked at her so tenderly, she wanted to weep. 'Sure we do.'

'How's your leg?'

'Fine.'

'You know you're crazy for coming in this condition.'

'Yeah.'

'But it's so good to see you.' She rubbed her cheek against his arm, but then another pain arrived. She'd been brave for hours and hours and hours. She couldn't turn into queen of the wimps now. Somehow, she had to be strong for a little longer.

'The sister says you're in transition.' Callum was strok-

ing her back softly. 'Breathe fast and shallow like we prac-
tised. Pant like Mac on a hot day.'

She was feeling very dizzy and ill. Worse than ever. Oh,
dear. She didn't want him to see her like this. She'd
planned to be so courageous. She tried to tell him she was
sorry, but a strange, noisy grunt broke from her lips. And
a completely new sensation crashed down on her. The bottom half of her body seemed to be straining away from
the rest of her.

'Aha!' she heard the midwife cry. 'I think your baby is
coming. You can start pushing now, Stella!'

She clutched Callum's hand. The midwife was doing
things to the end of her bed. Callum's free arm slipped
under her shoulders, supporting her, his voice close to her
ear. 'Good girl. At least I got here just in time for the best
part. It won't be long now.'

'Excellent. The head's crowning already,' the midwife
called.

Every cell in Stella's body was urging her to go with
this incredible force. There was nothing she could do but
push. In the slight lulls between contractions she sank
against Callum, exhausted and dreamy, sure that she had
no more strength, but then the urge to push was there
again, and she had no choice but to cooperate.

It was so much better now with Callum there. He didn't
let her give in to fear. 'You're doing so well, kiddo,' he
kept telling her. 'I can't wait to see your beautiful baby!'

The strain was becoming unbearable, but somehow,
with Callum and the midwife urging her on, Stella kept
pushing until at last she felt something warm and wobbly
between her legs.

'I can see the baby's head,' Callum told her.

There was no time to be scared.

'Keep pushing, Stella,' the midwife was calling, 'I'm

going to guide the shoulders out now.' To Callum, she said, 'If you help Stella up, she can see her baby being born.'

Did she want to see the baby? For a split second the old panic returned, but it was too late. Callum's arms were slipping lower down her back, helping her to lift away from the mattress, supporting her.

She looked down. And saw damp, dark, blood-smeared hair, a little red face with eyes tight shut, a little squashy nose and a tiny, tiny ruby-red mouth.

'Another push,' called the midwife.

'Deep breath,' reminded Callum, 'and then push! Go, Stella, that's the way. You little beauty! Here she comes. Oh, darling!'

'It's a girl!' cried the midwife.

Stella looked down again and saw her.

Saw a little red and perfect baby girl, her skin still shiny and wet.

She heard Callum's quiet exclamation. 'She's perfect!'

Trembling all over, she watched in awe as her baby experienced her first seconds of life: watched her tiny red hands uncurl, saw her fine, delicate fingers stretch and hit at the air, saw her dark wet hair plastered to her head in little curls. Before the midwife could start suctioning her, she heard her baby let out a gentle, inquisitive cry.

'It's Ruby!' Stella whispered.

Callum kissed her forehead. 'She's just beautiful, sweetheart.' His voice sounded as choked as she felt and it was so good to have his strong arm around her shoulders, still supporting her.

Stella saw the baby's little eyes open and blink then stare silently at the strange new world around her. 'She's gorgeous.' She couldn't believe this moment was really happening. This live, squirming baby was the wriggling bump she'd been carrying around for all those months. These were the little feet that had kicked against her ribs and had kept her awake at night.

This was her daughter. She was the mother of the cutest, most amazingly compact little girl. 'Hello, Ruby. I had no idea you'd be so sweet.'

Next minute the little face screwed up tight and the baby's lower lip trembled as she broke into a loud and lusty yell.

'Hey there, Ruby. No need to cry.' With the tip of her little finger, Stella reached to touch one tiny waving hand and she gasped with surprise as the baby's fingers instinctively closed tightly around her.

Ruby was drawing her very first breaths and yet her tiny hand was clinging to Stella, as if she already knew she was her mother, as if she needed her.

As if she knew her mother might leave her. *Would leave her!*

Stella couldn't believe the sudden swoop and rush of her emotions. Joy for this moment. Fear for the future. She looked up to Callum and saw his eyes swimming with bright tears.

It was too much! A painful swelling burst in her throat, her eyes stung and her heart raced. She heard a strangled moan breaking through her lips as she tried not to cry.

But the force was too strong.

She burst into tears.

Callum's fingers stroked the nape of her neck, then drew her head against him. She was crying for herself, for Ruby, for Callum…for Scott who would never see his baby…for her own mother. Oh, goodness, yes. She was crying for Marlene. She couldn't help thinking of her mother at this moment. Had Marlene felt this awe-filled wonder when she'd been born?

Stella felt as if she was crying for every mother and daughter who'd shared this precious moment of meeting for the very first time.

She clung to Callum and heard his heart pounding, as his arms enfolded her and he rocked her against his chest. She heard his soothing murmurs and felt him stroke her hair aside. His lips pressed against her forehead; she felt the warm wetness of his tears and couldn't hold back her loud heart-shattering sobs.

'You're a champion, Stell.'

'Oh, Callum,' she spluttered through her tears. 'I had no idea she'd be so beautiful.'

'Have you noticed?' he whispered. 'She has the cutest little toenails.'

She tried to smile but burst into more noisy sobs.

'This is a miracle,' she heard him tell the midwife.

'It always is,' came the reply.

'I mean, the fact that she's crying.'

'Oh?' The midwife sounded surprised, but then her manner turned matter-of-fact as she said to Stella, 'Let's put the babe to your breast, while I deal with the placenta.'

Stella's hospital gown was briskly pulled aside and, as Ruby was lifted up to her chest, she felt the skin-to-skin touch of her soft little body. She held her baby in her arms and the tiny mouth nuzzled her. And she fell helplessly, completely in love.

CHAPTER TWELVE

'RUBY'S twenty-four hours old, Callum. Do you think she's grown?'

He returned her broad smile. 'She's grown more beautiful,' he said and he meant it. The way he felt about Ruby was incredible. Ruby Roper. Scott's daughter. His daughter now. The sense of connection he felt to this tiny scrap of humanity was beyond anything he'd anticipated—almost mystical. Seeing her being born had been such a life-changing experience.

And Stella was looking so happy. Surrounded by dozens of flowers, she was wearing a glamorous, pale pink nightdress, a gift from his mother. He'd never seen her wearing anything so obviously feminine and she looked amazingly pretty and so proud as she gazed at the sleeping infant in the cot beside her. 'You love her, don't you?' he said.

'I'm crazy about her.'

He reached for her hand. 'I know I've said it before, but I'm so proud of you and I really am very grateful for the way you rescued me the other day.'

'I didn't do much.'

'You were fantastic the way you took charge and knew exactly who to ring and how. Anyone would think you'd lived in the bush all your life.'

She looked pleased. 'When Ruby's old enough, you'll have to teach her how to press that button on the telephone.'

Then her eyes suddenly lost their sparkle and Callum's heart sank to the bottom of his plaster cast. The wash of misery that clouded her face was all the evidence he needed. She was still planning to head off in a few weeks.

'Stella,' he said.

And at the same moment she said, 'Callum,' with her eyes downcast as she nervously smoothed the sheet over her legs. 'There's something I've been wanting to tell you.'

A giant fist squeezed his heart. Could he bear to hear what she had to say? 'I have something to tell you, too.'

'What is it?'

Fear held his tongue. 'Ladies first.'

'OK.' Closing her eyes, she spoke very quickly, 'I'm-not-going-to-London.'

It took a moment or two for her words to sink in and then he could hardly speak above the pounding of his heartbeats. 'Really?'

'I rang them and it's OK.'

'I see.' He shot a glance towards the tiny form in the crib. 'Now you've seen Ruby, you can't bear to leave her?'

'I made up my mind before I saw her—the day before she was born.'

His heart and lungs were doing crazy things. 'Uh-huh.'

'I had an attack of sanity in the plane when we were flying in here. I realised it would be irresponsible of me to head off to an important scientific position when I was so newly postnatal. I wouldn't be in the right frame of mind and I would let the team down.'

He nodded.

'As soon as I got you settled here in the hospital, I rang London and explained that I couldn't go. They were a bit put out, but they weren't overly worried. There are so many people queuing up for that job.'

'But—but how do you feel? It was such a big dream for you.'

She shrugged and smiled sadly. 'It's strange what can

happen to dreams. They can fade away until you can
hardly see them any more.'

'I see.' He wondered why he didn't feel better. Stella
wasn't going away. Why wasn't he ecstatic? Perhaps it had
something to do with the fact that she wasn't looking very
thrilled as she shared this news. What was missing from
all this?

'So do you agree that I did the right thing?' she asked.

He picked up her hand. It felt cold. 'If it's really what
you want.'

'I'll go back to Sydney instead,' she said.

'Sydney?' *Sydney?* A terrible mix of emotions clawed
at the back of his throat. 'Why—why Sydney?'

'My flatmate hasn't taken anyone else in, so I can go
back there and there's a good chance I can get a job back
in the office.'

Dropping her hand, he used the end of the bed for support to swing into an upright position and clumped away
from her clear across the room. There was something
mightily out of whack here. Stella was giving up her big
dream—her fantastic job in the UK for—for her old job
in *Sydney?*

'But what—what about—?' *What about Ruby? What
about us?* He wanted to shout.

*What about the way I feel about you? The way you wept
in my arms when Ruby was born? How can you just sail
off to Sydney after we shared all that?*

She looked as if she was holding her eyes extra wide to
keep from crying. 'What are you asking me?' she asked.
'What about—?'

'What about Ruby?'

Silvery tears sprang into her eyes. She sniffed and
dabbed at them with the backs of her hands. For what

seemed an age, she didn't answer and Callum almost forgot to breathe.

'I love Ruby so much,' she whispered, then her voice grew stronger as she continued, 'but when I accepted your proposal, I agreed that Ruby belongs on Birralee with you. You've kept your promises, Callum, so it would be rather selfish of me to start making new demands just because I'm not going to the northern hemisphere any more. I don't want to ruin Ruby's chance of a good family life. Or yours.'

'So you think you'll make our lives bright and beautiful by leaving us here and dashing off to Sydney?'

She didn't answer, but her chin lifted to that haughty angle that was so familiar to Callum and suddenly he *knew* she was trying to cover up how she really felt. He couldn't help grinning. 'Well, that actually makes things easier for me.'

'How?'

'If you race away from here and I have to come after you, the air fare to Sydney is a lot cheaper than a ticket to London.'

She looked puzzled. 'Come after me?'

'That's what I was going to tell you. If you insist on running away, I'm going to insist on coming after you and explaining a few important home truths. Of course, you could save us both a lot of effort if you let me explain them now.'

'What sort of home truths?

He hobbled back to the bed again. 'Let's start with the fact that you love me.'

Her mouth gaped. 'What makes you think that?'

'I have an intuition about these things.'

'Oh, yeah?' She sniffed again, reached for a tissue and blew her nose. 'Don't you remember? We had a business arrangement. You wanted to protect Scott's baby. You—you said our intimacy was a mistake. Falling in love was never part of your plan.'

'Maybe not, Stell, but it's happened anyhow, hasn't it?'

She stared at him, shaking her head with disbelief, but he could see hope shining through her tears.

Emboldened by that faint sign, he sat on the bed again, picked up her hand and placed it against the hammering in his chest. 'You see, you love me and Ruby. And we love you back. You've no idea how much we love you, Stell.'

More tears glistened, grew fat and spilled down her cheeks. 'Callum, you know about my background. I'm so afraid I have no idea what love really is.'

'But you've already admitted you love Ruby.'

'Yes,' she said. 'But a mother's love is spontaneous. It's unconditional. What makes you so sure I love you?'

He raised his free hand and traced the path of a tear with his thumb and then he bent close and gave her a sweet, slow kiss and she kissed him back just as sweetly, just as slowly. He smiled into her eyes. 'I've grown up surrounded by lots of happily married people, so I'm an expert. Believe me, I can tell you love me by the way you—' he paused and grinned '—by the way you look at me.'

'How do I look at you?'

'Like you can't wait to jump my bones. Like you can't wait to finish what we started the first time I painted your toenails.'

She blushed and rolled her eyes. 'That's not love. That's straight lust.'

'Well, let me put it another way. You force yourself to get up at the crack of dawn just so you can have breakfast with me. You've never been on a cattle station before, but you want to find out every darn thing there is to know about running my property.'

'Yes, but I'm a control freak.'

'And you like the idea of living with me and having me in your bed for the next forty, fifty maybe sixty years.'

She sucked in a surprised breath.

'You do, don't you?' he urged.

'What if I do? Aren't you still talking about lust?'

'No, Stell. That kind of staying power involves the other L word. The one you're so afraid of.'

She smiled shyly. 'I guess it might.'

'No doubt about it. Together for ever—just like we promised Reverend Shaw when we were married—that's how I see us.'

'Oh, Callum.'

He pressed his lips to her hand. 'I have this vision for Birralee that includes you and me as partners in every sense of the word…and Ruby and maybe two or three other little Rubies…'

Gathering her close, he kissed her again, showing her his love the best way he knew how. 'So if that's my version of love, how does it sound to you?'

He held his breath as he watched her face and saw her doubt give way to bright, shining joy.

'It sounds like the dream that shoved London out of my head,' she whispered. 'And it sounds as if I'm going to be absolutely, totally, up to my eyebrows in love for the rest of my life.'

Blissful seconds passed as their eyes lingered and they absorbed each other's happiness and felt at long last a beautiful peace entering their hearts.

Stella couldn't resist scattering a shower of happy little kisses all over Callum's face, his neck and finally she settled for his wonderful mouth.

'Callum, I don't think you have any idea how drop-dead gorgeous you are.'

Sudden shyness tilted his smile.

'I've been wanting to tell you things like that for so long.'

His hands caressed her shoulders through the soft fabric of her nightie. 'If anyone's drop-dead gorgeous it's you, sweetheart.'

Stella laughed softly as she tightened her arms around his neck and nipped his lower lip softly between her teeth. 'I should warn you, I'm very susceptible to flattery.'

His answering laugh was playful, rippling with happiness. 'And I've been meaning to tell you what a sexy mouth you have. And your hair. I love your silky hair. As for your—'

'Toenails?'

'Them, too,' Callum said. 'Sexiest toenails in the whole damn world.'

And of course, they had to kiss again.

'Just as well you have a private room,' came a voice from the doorway.

Stella looked over Callum's shoulder to see a smiling nurse standing there. 'Mrs Roper, your parents-in-law are in reception and they wish to know if you're receiving visitors.'

'Oh,' she cried. Her eyes sought Callum's and he nodded. 'Yes, of course.'

As the nurse left, Stella took a deep happy breath and sank back against the pillows. 'They'll love Ruby, won't they?'

He grinned and leaned forward to kiss the tip of her nose. 'They'll adore her. They'll want to spoil her rotten.'

Stella's face grew serious. 'Callum, I'd like to tell them the truth—that she's Scott's baby.' The idea hit her suddenly and she knew instantly that it was important to her long-term happiness to get everything out in the open with Callum's family.

He frowned. 'I don't know if they're ready for it.'

She reached for his hand, linked her fingers with his and squeezed. 'It'll be OK when they understand how much we love each other and how much we both love Ruby... I think we should trust them to cope, Callum. They're Ropers. They're the same as you—intelligent, compassionate and tough.'

Footsteps were approaching down the corridor. Callum's hand tightened around hers. 'You're braver than I am about this, but I suspect you're right.'

Margaret and the Senator hesitated when they reached the doorway, but the minute they saw Callum and Stella together, their faces broke into joyful smiles.

'Hello! Do come in,' Stella cried keeping Callum's hand firmly clasped in hers. 'It's so good you got here safely. Come and see our darling little girl.'

They hurried forward eagerly. 'Stella, dear, you look so well.'

'Congratulations!'

'Oh, look at her! Isn't she the sweetest little duck!'

Stella and Callum had to separate and submit to hugs and kisses. Ruby slept through all the noise while she was admired extravagantly. Margaret wept happy tears. Senator Roper kept thumping Callum on the back. Everyone grinned broadly.

After the first excitement settled down, the Senator stood beside the crib and stared at Ruby. 'Who does Ruby look like—Stella or Callum?'

Stella's heartbeats raced as she watched him study her daughter's little cap of fuzzy light brown hair, the hint of a dimple in her chin and her turned up nose.

Her hand sought Callum's again. 'I think she looks like her father,' she said softly and she felt Callum's grip tighten like a vice around her fingers.

'Do you?' Margaret frowned. 'I can't really see much resemblance to Callum.'

'No,' Stella said. She had to do this. She *had* to do it. She couldn't go on living a lie for another minute. 'But don't you think she looks a little like Scott?'

'*Scott?*' came Margaret's astonished cry.

Then there was total silence. The room seemed to swim as Stella watched their shocked faces. Callum's hand was gripping hers so tightly her fingers felt numb.

She dared to look at him and his face was so stony it might have been carved from granite. But his eyes shimmered with tears and were riveted on her. Lifting a trembling hand, she touched his cheek.

Then she looked at his mother's pale face, at his father's dark glare and she took a deep breath. 'Ruby is Scott's daughter.'

As soon as the words were out, Stella felt sure that her strength and courage would desert her. She felt dizzy as stunned exclamations and gasps of shocked amazement circled around her. Tears threatened. These days she was getting very good at crying.

'What I want you to know,' she said as steadily as she could, 'is that Callum has been very gallant.' She did her best to swallow the pain that was filling her throat. 'As soon as he knew that I was expecting Scott's baby, he offered me his hand in marriage, so that—so that Ruby could be a legitimate member of your family.'

'I see,' whispered Margaret. She shot worried glances to her husband, to Callum and back to Stella.

There was a horrible, painful, awkward silence and

Stella wished she could crawl into a hole and stay hidden for a decade or two.

Then Callum cleared his throat. 'Actually Stella's account of what happened isn't quite accurate,' he said. 'Sure, I wanted to keep Scott's baby in the family, but marrying her wasn't a matter of gallantry at all.' He raised the hand he'd been crushing so fiercely and pressed it to his lips as he sent her a smouldering smile. 'I wanted to make Stella mine from the first minute I saw her. One smile from her and I became twice the man I was before.'

A little cry escaped Stella.

'I happen to love her very much,' Callum told his parents. 'And it seems that, by some miracle, she loves me.'

'I certainly do.' Stella looked straight at the Senator knowing she'd never felt so sure of anything or as happy as she did at this moment.

'Marrying Stella is the best, the very best thing I've ever done,' Callum continued. 'You can be sure that Ruby will grow up on Birralee surrounded by love.'

'Oh!' cried Margaret, tears streaming down her face as she rushed forward to hug them again.

At that moment a lusty little cry erupted from the crib. Everyone looked at everyone else.

Callum's father was closest to the crib and, after a moment's hesitation, he leaned forward and lifted the baby gingerly. They watched as he stood there, holding tiny Ruby awkwardly while he stared down into her little face.

Stella steeled herself for the Senator's reaction to her bombshell. It seemed they were all waiting for him to say something.

He cleared his throat. 'I'm overjoyed to be welcoming this very precious little girl into our family.' His Adam's apple worked hard in his throat and his eyes gleamed as he dropped a gentle kiss on Ruby's forehead, then smiled at Stella. 'Thank you, Stella, for bringing Scott's daughter to us.'

'Yes,' cried Margaret, and she gripped Stella's hand. 'Thank you so much, you dear girl. Thank you for Ruby.' Her other hand shook as she reached with it to grasp Callum's, so that the three of them were linked. 'And thank you for making Callum so happy.'

Stella smiled at them all through her tears. Thank you, she wanted to say. Thank you for becoming my family. But she'd said as much as she could manage for now. The rest could come later.

For now she couldn't believe she was so lucky.

There were more happy tears as Ruby was passed to Margaret for a grandmotherly cuddle and then to Stella. Callum was on his feet and he and his father were shaking hands, then clasping each other.

Ruby's cries grew stronger and Callum and his parents went outside so that Stella could feed her baby in peace. She was tucking her back into the crib when she heard the clump, clump of Callum's crutches. He looked very pleased as he came into the room.

'You were right, my clever girl, it was good to get everything out in the open,' he said. 'Those parents of mine are over the moon.'

'About everything?'

'About absolutely everything.' With another clump, clump he crossed the room and took her in his arms. 'Oh, Stella, you've no idea how happy I am, too. I'm so very much in love with you.'

'I love you more,' she said and she smiled into his eyes. Wrapped in happiness, she clung to him, marvelling at her good fortune. 'You told your parents that you wanted me from the first moment you saw me,' she whispered.

'It's true. I did. I fell head over heels in love with you

at that party in Sydney and I've been helplessly in love with you ever since.'

'Same here.'

He pulled away slightly to study her. 'You're joking.'

'No, Callum. I wouldn't joke about that. The minute you walked into that room it was as if someone had let off sky-rockets inside me.'

'But you rejected me.'

'Because I was frightened,' she admitted, wondering how she could have ever been so foolish. 'I didn't know how to deal with the strong feelings you roused in me.'

'You're not frightened any more, are you?'

'Only a little.'

'Oh, Stell,' he whispered hoarsely, 'don't be frightened.' With one finger beneath her chin, he tipped her face so that he could look directly into her glistening eyes. 'My darling, I'm the one who should be terrified. Don't you know the power you have over me? You hold my heart in your hands.'

This time they were both trembling as they kissed. And Stella knew they were both thinking of the long nights yet to come and the bedroom they would share when they went home with Ruby to Birralee.

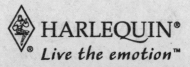

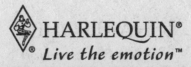

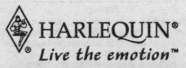

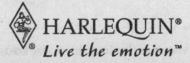

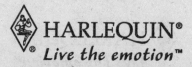

HARLEQUIN®
INTRIGUE®

Our unique brand of high-caliber romantic suspense just cannot be contained. And to meet our readers' demands, Harlequin Intrigue is expanding its publishing lineup to include **SIX** breathtaking titles every month!

Here's what we have in store for you:

❏ A trilogy of **Heartskeep** stories by Dani Sinclair

❏ More great **Bachelors at Large** books featuring sexy, single cops

❏ Plus outstanding contributions from your favorite Harlequin Intrigue authors, such as Amanda Stevens, B.J. Daniels and Gayle Wilson

MORE variety.
MORE pulse-pounding excitement.
MORE of your favorite authors and series.
Every month.

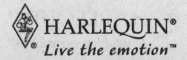

HARLEQUIN®
® *Live the emotion*™